KIRSTY MURRAY was born in Melbourne, the middle child in a family of seven kids. After several years of travel, she returned to Melbourne where she lives in a big chaotic household with her partner and a gang of teenagers.

Praise for *Walking Home with Marie-Claire*:

A really adventurous and exciting book with lots of surprises. *Meghan Jennings and Kaitlyn McLeod, year 6*

I couldn't put it down! *Hilary Martin, aged 14*

Murray captures well the immediate spark and ferocious intensity of childhood friendships.
Sydney Morning Herald

A good mix of deep, thought-provoking moments, and fun. *Reading Time*

Other books by Kirsty Murray

Fiction
Zarconi's Magic Flying Fish
Market Blues
Bridie's Fire
(Book one in *Children of the Wind*)

Non-fiction
Howard Florey Miracle Maker
Tough Stuff: true stories about kids and courage

KIRSTY MURRAY

Walking Home
with
Marie-Claire

ALLEN&UNWIN

First published in 2002

Copyright © Kirsty Murrray 2002

Allen & Unwin
83 Alexander St
Crows Nest NSW 2065
Australia
Phone: (61 2) 8425 0100
Fax: (61 2) 9906 2218
Email: info@allenandunwin.com
Web: www.allenandunwin.com

National Library of Australia
Cataloguing-in-Publication entry:

Murray, Kirsty.
Walking home with Marie-Claire.

For children aged 10-14 years.
ISBN 1 86508 546 4.

1. School children - Juvenile fiction. 2. Nineteen
seventies - Juvenile fiction. 3. Children - Conduct of
life - Juvenile fiction. 4. Draft resisters - Juvenile
fiction. I. Title.

A823.3

Designed by Jo Hunt
Set in 11 on 14.5pt Janson by Midland Typesetters
Printed by McPherson's Printing Group

10 9 8 7 6 5 4 3 2

Acknowledgements

Thanks to Romanie Harper and May Maloney for their supportive feedback and to Ros Price, Sarah Brenan and Penni Russon for their wise words. Also thanks to Ken Harper, Julian Golby and Terry Miller for helping me revisit the 1970s, and to Mary Hoyle for sharing the upside-down days.

For Romanie Ellen Harper, with love

Contents

I

Miss Julia's Pony Club

Pauline finished colouring in the centre of the last 'o' on page 26 of her English book and looked up as the classroom door swung open. The principal, Mr Brown, came in with a new girl. Black-eyed, honey-skinned, with long dark hair in two thick braids, she stood at the front of the room and gazed at the class with casual defiance.

'Grade Six B, this is Margaret Tierney, and I'd like you all to make her feel welcome here at Wellington Street Primary.'

'My name's not Margaret. It's Marie-Claire,' said the girl.

Mr Brown looked startled. 'I beg your pardon, Margaret.' Everyone knew that you never talked back to Mr Brown, even if he was wrong. Especially if he was wrong.

'Marie-Claire. It's French.'

Mr Brown looked flustered. 'Yes, well, Marie-Claire, at Wellington Street Primary, we speak respectfully to our elders.'

'Yes, sir. I understand, sir,' said Marie-Claire. Mr Brown frowned and looked out over the classroom, as if he was about to deliver a lecture but then thought better of it. He nodded stiffly to Mrs Box, and quickly left the room. There was a buzz of suppressed excitement as the door shut behind him.

Mrs Box gestured the new girl towards the empty seat beside Pauline.

'If you don't mind,' said the girl, 'I'd rather sit by myself. Could I have that desk over there?'

All eyes focused in amazement on Marie-Claire. Obviously, she had a lot to learn about fitting in with teachers. Mrs Box glared at Pauline as if she was somehow responsible and then gave in, waving Marie-Claire towards the back of the room with an impatient gesture. A flurry of conversations broke out.

Pauline knew she was blushing. She pressed the palms of her hands against her cheeks to try and take the heat out of them and stared hard at her exercise book. She hated the way her whole body could flush pink so easily. It came with having red hair. It wasn't as if she cared where the new girl sat.

Melinda and Jenny turned around in their desks to stare at the girl.

'Phew, that was close,' whispered Jenny.

'We are so lucky she didn't wind up sitting next to you,' said Melinda, leaning close to Pauline.

'She might be okay,' said Pauline. 'I wouldn't mind.'

Melinda and Jenny both looked hurt. 'I had to sit by myself all through Grade Four,' said Jenny. 'And Melinda did it for Grade Five. We all agreed it was your turn this year.'

'But she's new.'

'We don't need anyone new,' said Melinda. 'Besides, she looks like a dag.'

Mrs Box barked out an order and raised her hand for the class to be silent. Jenny and Melinda quickly turned around to face the front. Pauline glanced across at the new girl. She was wearing a pair of blue jeans and a faded grey jumper. In front of her was a brand new exercise book where she'd written her name, *Marie-Claire Tierney*, in fancy curling letters. No one else in the whole school had two names. As Mrs Box droned on at the front of the classroom, Pauline started to doodle. *Pauline Janet McArdle*, she scrawled all over the page in front of her, but somehow it didn't have quite the same style as *Marie-Claire*, no matter how many decorative bits and fancy scrolls she added to it. She tore the page out and threw it into her desk.

At morning recess, everyone crowded around the stacked crates of milk outside the classroom. Beads of moisture glistened on the small glass bottles and the milk was warm and slightly sour from having been left in the spring sunshine. Scott Collins took a mouthful, then ran to the sink outside the artroom and spat it out. But Marie-Claire took a bottle and sculled it, opening her mouth and tipping it back. She looked around at the group of startled faces and laughed. Then she wiped the white moustache of milk from her lip with the back of her hand and walked away.

'She's mental,' said Scott.

Heat rose up from the bitumen in shimmering waves. Crowds of little kids milled around the drinking fountains, splashing their hands in the steel trough. Out on the playing field, boys were kicking a football in a cloud of grey dust. Melinda and Jenny sat on the bench in the shade of a peppercorn tree, waiting for Pauline to join them. Pauline lingered at the drinking fountains, wishing recess didn't always have to be so boring.

As she bent over to take a drink, a tiny fair-haired girl ran across the playground towards the little kids at the water taps.

'They're making up a really grouse game just for us!' she said in a breathless lisp. 'Up in the shelter shed. Quick!'

The gang of small kids streamed across the yard towards the back shelter shed. Pauline glanced across at Melinda and Jenny and was relieved to see them engrossed in conversation. She walked quickly after the trail of Preppies.

An obstacle course was set out inside the shelter shed.

Branches, brooms and bits of wood had been dragged in from all over the schoolyard. A fence paling had been laid across two rubbish bins, and standing next to the arrangement was the new girl, Marie-Claire. She had a switch in one hand, and a motley assortment of Preppies and Grade One kids swarmed around her.

'Line up, line up,' she cried, slapping her thigh with the switch of willow. 'Miss Julia's pony club is about to begin training. What lucky ponies you are! Only the best ponies in the world are allowed to be in my school.'

Small kids darted forward like sparrows, elbowing their way into the line-up. Pauline stood in the doorway, watching as 'Miss Julia' organised her ponies. One by one, the little kids rushed at the barriers. Whenever one of them reached the end of the obstacle course, Marie-Claire rewarded them with a pat on the head and a lump of sugar.

A small boy stumbled and fell as he struggled to clear the jump. He came down hard on the concrete floor, skinning his knee.

'Up, my beauty,' cried Marie-Claire, standing over the boy with her riding crop.

Pauline watched disbelievingly as the boy neighed pathetically, staggered to his feet, and limped to the back of the line, determined to brave the jump again.

Suddenly Marie-Claire looked across at Pauline.

'You wanna play?'

'It doesn't look like a lot of fun to me. I don't think any of these kids really want to play this game.'

'No one's forcing them,' said Marie-Claire. She stared at Pauline, her dark eyes fierce and compelling. Pauline had seen a man on TV who could twist spoons with his eyes. For a moment, she could imagine all sorts of things contorting into weird shapes under Marie-Claire's gaze.

The little kids shifted restlessly from foot to foot, waiting for 'Miss Julia' to tell them what to do next.

'Go away,' one of the small girls shouted at Pauline. 'You're wrecking our game.'

Pauline turned and walked out of the shelter shed into the bright sunshine.

2

Truth or dare

Pauline always walked home alone. No one else in her grade had ever lived on the far side of the railway tracks, until now.

Marie-Claire walked a few metres ahead of Pauline, her schoolbag slapping rhythmically against her thigh. Her long dark braids swung back and forward as she walked.

Melinda and Jenny had spent a lot of the afternoon passing notes to Pauline about the new girl. Melinda's note said it was pathetic Marie-Claire hadn't bothered to come to school in uniform. Jenny's said Marie-Claire must have flunked a year at her old school because she was so much taller than the other girls. Pauline drew patterns around the edge of the notes and shrugged when Melinda and Jenny turned around with questioning expressions, waiting for replies. She hadn't sent an answer. She couldn't make up her mind what she thought about Marie-Claire.

At the bottom of Wellington Street, a long row of boys were sitting on the high brick wall that surrounded the playground of Sacre Coeur Catholic school. The boys started chanting 'Proddy frogs, stink like dogs' as the girls approached. Pauline was used to the jeering, but she had never got used to the stones that rained down along with the words. She thought about turning back to take the long way home – and then saw that Marie-Claire was already in their line of fire.

Pauline hitched her schoolbag onto her shoulder. 'Run!' she said as she drew level with Marie-Claire.

'No! That's what they want,' Marie-Claire said, grabbing Pauline by the arm. 'Act like you don't care.'

Pauline slowed her pace and fell in step with Marie-Claire. A stone landed on the ground right in front of them and Marie-Claire picked it up and slipped it into her pocket. Then she waved at the gang of bewildered boys and casually walked on without looking back.

'Wow!' said Pauline. She glanced back over her shoulder. The boys were watching them with puzzled expressions. 'That was great. They look gobsmacked!'

'You have to call their bluff. You can make people believe anything if you believe it yourself. My mother taught me that. She was a famous actress. She could make the audience believe anything she wanted. But then she fell in love with my father and they had me and of course I'm more important to her than anything so she stopped acting.'

Pauline wasn't sure what to do with this information.

'What if those boys had kept chucking rocks and one of them had hit us?' she asked. 'What if they'd jumped down off the wall and come and beat us up? What would you have done then?'

'But they didn't, did they? It's like truth or dare. And I always go for dare.'

They reached the railway crossing just as the bells started ringing. Pauline stopped but Marie-Claire sauntered straight onto the tracks, ignoring the lowered boom gates. She bent over to check her shoelace, not even looking up when the train whistle blew. Pauline felt the bitumen vibrating beneath her feet. A sickening swell of panic rose up in her throat. She gripped the safety rail and stared at Marie-Claire, willing her to run. The train hurtled towards her.

'Oi, ya stupid kid, get off the line!' shouted a motorist, putting his head out of his car window.

Marie-Claire gave him the rude finger and leapt over the safety rail on the other side just as the train roared through the crossing. When the train had passed, Marie-Claire was out of sight.

The man in the car called out to Pauline as he drove through the railway crossing.

'You know that girl?'

He didn't wait for an answer.

'She wants a belting,' he shouted and drove off.

Pauline couldn't imagine anyone laying a hand on Marie-Claire. They'd have to catch her first.

3

It's time

The doorbell rang and Pauline went to answer it. Even though the frosted glass panel distorted the shape, she could tell the visitor was Julie, her brother Brian's girlfriend.

When she opened the door, Julie smiled a wide, white smile, but Pauline blushed. Julie's breasts were exactly level with her face. Maybe that's why they always looked so huge. Or maybe it was because there was always a slogan emblazoned across her T-shirt. This one had 'IT'S TIME', in fat, wonky lettering.

'What's it time for?' asked Pauline.

'Don't you watch TV, Pauline? Haven't you seen that ad, you know, the one where Little Patti's singing *It's time for a change, yeah it's time, time for living, time for loving, it's time for a change, yeah it's time*?' She mimed the dance steps as she sang the jingle. Pauline watched Julie's feet.

It was embarrassing to have to look at the way her T-shirt stretched even further out of shape. 'The Labor Party is going to win this election. Isn't it fantastic! By the time you're in high school, there'll be a Labor government in power for the first time in our lives!'

Pauline tried to look politely interested.

'You look like your mother when you pull that face,' said Julie. 'Listen, honey, if you're not part of the solution, you're part of the problem. Is Brian home?'

Pauline shrugged and stepped aside. Julie went straight to Brian's room, letting out a swirl of incense and cigarette smoke as she shut the door behind her. Pauline tiptoed to the closed door and pressed her ear against it. She could hear the sound of music and someone singing about a 'peace train'. Before Julie came along, Pauline had spent a lot of time hanging around in Brian's room. She would lie on his bed while he studied, flipping through his comic-book collection and chatting about anything and everything. Now, even though Brian was still always nice to her, it wasn't the same. He was always either with Julie or out at a meeting or a rally. She never had him all to herself anymore.

Pauline pushed open the swing door to the kitchen. Mum was standing at the table, peeling vegetables onto a sheet of newspaper. Dad sat by the window, hands around his evening beer, talking. They didn't notice Pauline slip in and sit on the stool at the other end of the table.

'They're not going to chase him now,' said Dad. 'The troops have been coming home since last year. They're not going to send him OS. The boy's making a show, that's all.'

'It's that Jezebel. She's put him up to it,' said Mum with bitterness.

'Now don't you go blaming Julie. Brian was taking himself off to those anti-Vietnam marches long before he met her.'

Pauline remembered going to one of those marches with Brian. She'd promised never to tell Mum and Dad. Brian was meant to be baby-sitting her while Mum and Dad were at a bowls championship, but instead he'd taken her on the train into the city and then put her up on his shoulders to see the crowds, thousands and thousands of people waving banners and placards all the way along Bourke Street.

'Is Brian going to join the army?' asked Pauline.

Dad glanced up, startled. 'And how long have you been sitting there, missy?'

'I said is Brian going to Vietnam?' she asked again, crossly. It was so annoying, the way Dad never bothered to answer her questions.

'Brian's not going anywhere, love,' said Mum, not looking up from her vegetable peelings. 'It's just that his number's come up in the draft and he has to do his National Service.'

'And by God, he's going to do it,' said Dad.

The swing door flew open and Brian and Julie came into the kitchen, arm-in-arm.

'Hey, Doug. Hey, Lorraine,' said Brian, nodding at Mum and Dad.

Pauline winced and waited for the fight to begin.

'I've told you before, boy, I don't like it when you call your mother and me by our first names. It's disrespectful. I never called my mother and father anything but Mum and Dad. Showed I knew my place with them, and I'd appreciate if you did likewise.'

Brian sighed impatiently and ran one hand through his long hair.

'Look, folks, I thought you ought to know, I've got my medical tomorrow but I'm going to tear up the papers right in front of them.'

Dad shook his head.

'My own son,' he said disbelievingly.

'Come on, Brian,' said Mum. 'You don't want to do something like that. You've always been the sort of young man who does the right thing. And besides, it won't be for very long. You'll be home again before you know it.'

'I *am* about to do the right thing, Mum.'

'Not in my books,' said Dad fiercely.

Mum wiped her hands on her apron and looked anxiously from her husband to her son.

'If you're really nervous about it, love, you could always try applying for one of those exemptions,' said Mum.

'Mum, I'm not nervous. I'm not doing this because I'm frightened! Julie's brother Tom risked prison for what he believed in. That's the sort of guts I admire, not all those mugs that just do what they're told and go and get their heads blown off fighting a stupid, senseless war. Now Tom's in hiding, and you know what? His mother has joined Save Our Sons and is out there campaigning to do away with National Service. She has the guts to support her son because she understands he's doing the right thing.'

Mum flushed pink and looked away as if he'd hit her.

'Don't you take that tone with your mother,' said Dad, slamming one hand down on the table. 'Your mother and me, we did our bit for this country. I don't see why you can't do the same.'

Brian's face grew sullen. 'I've told you before, there's a moral issue at stake. I'm not allowed to vote until I'm twenty-one, but I can be sent to Vietnam to be killed.'

'But you won't have to go to Vietnam or anywhere else. The troops are coming home!' said Mum, imploring.

The argument grew fiercer and Pauline retreated, slipping out the back door and across the lawn to her favourite hiding-place, up the apple tree in the back garden. The blossom had finished and hard green apples, no bigger than marbles, were taking shape on the tree. Pauline picked one and took a bite of the bitter fruit. She could still hear the shouting. She'd never seen Brian this angry before. Mum and Pauline's big sister, Sue, had terrible rows where they both yelled the house down but Brian and Mum had never, ever fought. If Pauline shut her eyes she could remember how it used to be, with everyone talking as if they really liked each other. When did they become this sort of family?

When the mosquitoes got so thick that Pauline tired of swatting them, she went back inside. The argument was still raging, having moved from the kitchen to the front of the house.

Julie was standing on the verandah, her face averted, while Mum and Dad stood either side of Brian on the front doorstep.

'I don't have to take this bull crap from you anymore,' Brian shouted.

'If you leave this house now,' Dad yelled back, 'don't think for one minute that you'll be welcome back.'

'That's it,' hissed Brian. 'I'm out of here.' He stepped out the front door and slammed it shut. A long crack, like forked lightning, appeared across the pane of frosted glass.

4

PJ forever

Pauline found the newspaper spread out on the pale blue laminex of the kitchen table. She sprinkled sugar on her cornflakes and sat down to read. There he was, her own brother, being led down the steps of the courthouse. Her own brother on page 7 of the morning paper, staring straight into the cameras. He looked so handsome and important. It gave her a weird feeling, as if she couldn't really be related to him anymore.

Underneath, the caption read: 'Brian McArdle being led from the courthouse after being sentenced to 21 days for resisting the draft and tearing up his medical certificate.'

Carefully, Pauline tore the page out, folded it into a square and put it in her schoolbag. She put her head around her parents' bedroom door to say goodbye to Mum, who'd gone back to bed after Sue and Dad left, saying she had a headache. She'd had a lot of headaches since Brian left home.

Pauline walked fast, her legs flashing out in front of her. She hated her short dress. It was one of Sue's old ones and the hem was starting to fray, but Mum said there was no point buying a new one so late in the year. Soon she'd inherit Sue's old high-school uniforms, faded to a sickly pale green. They'd probably be way too short for her as well. Sue liked to take up the hem on everything, to show off her long, long legs that went on forever and looked great in anything. Pauline would much rather have worn jeans, like Marie-Claire. Funny how brothers and sisters could be so different. Brian had the brains and the handsome face, and Sue had the gorgeous blonde hair and spunky good looks. Pauline was stuck with the leftover bits – red hair, freckles, pale eyes and shyness. Sometimes Sue told her she was stubborn just like their mother, but it didn't sound like much of a compliment.

As she neared the railway, she saw Marie-Claire, sitting on a low cream brick wall, plucking daisies from a bush and threading them into a chain.

'You'd better hurry. Didn't you hear the bell?' asked Pauline. 'We're going to be really late.'

'It's too hot for school today,' said Marie-Claire. 'Let's wag.'

Pauline stared at her.

'What if they phone our parents?'

Marie-Claire laughed.

'Who cares? We could go on a big adventure if we wag. That's better than anything that happens in boring old school.'

'Hmm,' said Pauline. They were already so late, they'd be sent to the principal for sure. Melinda and Jenny would be pissed off at her for not being on time, too. It would mean she'd be banned from collecting the tuckshop orders and they'd have to do it without her. But if they found out she'd wagged with Marie-Claire, they'd think she was a real traitor. She looked down the road that led to the school and then back at Marie-Claire.

'What if I get sprung, walking around in my uniform and all?'

'Don't worry,' said Marie-Claire. 'We'll go places where no one will ask us anything, and if they do we'll just make something up. Come on.' She turned onto the narrow overgrown path that ran beside the railway line. It was cooler in the shade, away from the shimmering morning heat. As they walked, Marie-Claire picked a handful of sourgrass with pale yellow flowers and chewed on the stalks.

'You know, we could live in the wild.' She grabbed a handful of fennel leaves. 'Try this stuff. It's what they make licorice from. I've boiled it down in a big vat at home and turned it into aniseed balls. We could be like the kid in that film *My Side of the Mountain*, except it would be like our side of the city. And we'd sort of live like wild children and no one would find us. We'd be invisible right here in Melbourne.'

Pauline looked at her and laughed.

They stopped under a shady peppercorn tree, and sat down in the long grass. Marie-Claire reached over and unzipped Pauline's schoolbag, pulling things out one at a time.

'What are you doing?' said Pauline, trying to grab her bag back.

'Calm down. I'm just looking. Checking the supplies.'

One of the first things she pulled out was the page from the newspaper with Brian's picture on it. She unfolded it and smoothed it out on her lap.

'Why have you got this?' she asked.

'That's my big brother, in the picture,' said Pauline, tearing up a blade of grass and shredding it, not looking up.

Marie-Claire read the article and then refolded it, putting it back inside Pauline's schoolbag without saying anything.

'My brother says the Vietnam War is really stupid and Australia shouldn't be in it. He's really big on politics and that sort of stuff. You got any brothers or sisters?' asked Pauline.

Marie-Claire took a while to answer. 'I had a big brother once. He was a champion horseman. He rode a big black stallion and he used to pick me up from my old school every day and we'd go riding through the bush together. He'd put both his arms around me and we'd ride for hours and hours.'

'So does he still live in the country or something?'

'He's dead,' replied Marie-Claire, looking away. 'He died in Vietnam.'

Pauline stared at Marie-Claire, dumbstruck. Somehow, having a brother in prison couldn't compare with having a brother in the grave. And she'd said the Vietnam War was stupid! She could feel her cheeks burning with shame.

Marie-Claire started rummaging through Pauline's bag again, pulling out her lunchbox, schoolbooks and finally the crumpled piece of paper that Pauline had scrawled her signature on.

'What's this? Pauline Janet McArdle? Is that your proper name?'

'Yeah. I know, it's daggy. So what?'

'So how about we call you PJ? PJ McArdle. Makes you sound like a famous reporter or an American sports star or something like that.'

'Sounds like a boy's name to me.'

'You got a problem with that?'

'PJ McArdle,' Pauline said slowly, testing it out. 'No, I think I like it.'

They spent the whole morning walking and talking, following the railway line down to the sea. On the way, Pauline took a one-cent piece out of her pocket and laid it on the hot silver track. After the 11.42 had sped past, they ran to pick up the flattened coin.

'We could have killed someone doing that,' said Marie-Claire as Pauline examined the distorted image of the possum, spread into a weird shape across the coin.

'How do you mean?' asked Pauline.

'I heard this story, about some kid who put a bunch of twenty-cent pieces on the tracks once and derailed an entire train – hundreds of people got killed. Some rich kid, showing off. The whole train skidded off the tracks and rolled over and over. He got crushed to death too.'

'You sure know a lot of stories.'

'Yeah, well, I like to listen. When I was little, I used to sit under the kitchen table and just listen to the stuff the grown-ups talked about.'

'Me too,' said Pauline. ''Cept they never say anything very interesting in my house.'

When they reached the beach, she shared her packed lunch with Marie-Claire. They took off their shoes and paddled in the sea and practised skimming stones out across the water.

PJ watched a flat grey stone bounce seven times across the shimmering blue sea and each time the stone bounced, she felt her heart leap with pleasure. She turned to look at Marie-Claire, but Marie-Claire was standing at the mouth of a big stormwater drain further down the beach, peering into the darkness.

'Hey, Pauline,' called Marie-Claire.

'Not Pauline,' said PJ as she joined her at the mouth of the drain. 'PJ from now on. PJ forever.'

Marie-Claire grinned. 'So, PJ, are you game for an adventure?'

PJ followed Marie-Claire's gaze, into the mouth of the huge dark tunnel.

'Isn't it kind of dangerous, messing around in storm-water drains?'

'See!' said Marie-Claire triumphantly. 'I knew you were thinking what I was thinking!'

'But we don't have a torch or anything,' said PJ. 'And my dad always says these drains can flood really fast. He's a plumber and he knows about that sort of stuff.'

'It'll be grouse. We could explore all under the city just by following the drains. Come on, I dare ya.'

A shallow flow of water from the drain eddied around their ankles as they walked into the darkness. The sound of the splashing water echoed as they waded through the water, deeper into the tunnel. Blackness folded in around them. PJ looked back over her shoulder and saw the sea as a small, bright circle of blue. 'Marie-Claire, are you still there? Let's turn back.'

'But we could be getting somewhere really interesting.'

'It's too dark. I can't see you anymore.'

'I'm right beside you.'

'Why are we whispering?'

'I don't know,' replied Marie-Claire.

'The water's rising,' said PJ. 'Don't you think the water's rising?'

'You're imagining it,' said Marie-Claire.

'But it's up to my knees,' said PJ urgently.

Suddenly, Marie-Claire stopped and grabbed PJ's hand.

'What's that noise?'

It hit PJ so hard, it knocked the breath right out of her. She was thrown forward into the swirling water and then swept up hard against the wall of the drain. Marie-Claire's hand was wrenched from hers as the surging water forced her under. She thrashed her way to the crest of the flood, and saw the circle of light at the mouth of the drain spiralling towards her. Next moment, she was sweeping out to sea.

A long strand of seaweed twisted itself around her throat and she clawed it away. *This is how kids drown*, she thought. *We'll both be swept out to sea and my family will never know, 'cause they'll never find my body.* She began swimming frantically across the flow of drainwater.

Marie-Claire's dark head broke the surface not far from PJ.

'Hey, we can stand up here,' she called. PJ sighed with relief as her feet touched the sand and they began wading ashore.

'Wow,' said Marie-Claire, wringing the water from her long hair. 'That was wild!'

'It was really dangerous. We could have drowned!'

'But we didn't,' said Marie-Claire, grinning.

'Well, my dad would kill me if he knew I'd done that.'

They walked slowly back up the beach and sat down in the warm sand beside their schoolbags. Their wet clothes clung to their skin.

'We have to do something to remember this moment forever,' said Marie-Claire, solemnly.

'I don't think I'm going to forget it in a hurry,' said PJ, pushing a handful of wet hair away from her face.

Marie-Claire reached over to her schoolbag. She ripped a page out of the back of an exercise book and wrote in her fanciest lettering: *On this day, December 1, 1972, we, the undersigned, have shared our first big adventure and swear undying loyalty to each other.*

'What do you reckon?' she asked, handing the paper to PJ.

PJ giggled when she read it. 'Okay, give me the pen and I'll sign.'

'No, not with a pen. It's a sacred document, so you have to sign it in blood.'

'In blood?'

Marie-Claire wriggled around trying to get her hand into her wet jeans pocket. She pulled out a small pocket knife. Then she slashed the tip of her index finger. Thick dark blood oozed out and ran down the lines in her hand.

'Give it here,' she said. She signed her name in big looping letters – *Marie-Claire Tierney*. Her finger bled so much that little flecks of blood spattered the paper.

PJ hesitated. Once she'd tried to talk Melinda and Jenny into being her blood sisters, but they had said it was a disgusting idea and only tomboys did things like that. Marie-Claire held the knife out towards her, waiting. Wincing, PJ cut into the soft wet skin of her forefinger. A tiny drop of blood appeared. She managed to make a shaky looking *P* and then, by squeezing her finger as hard as she could, enough blood oozed out to form a *J*.

Marie-Claire smiled and took back the 'document'. Her finger was still bleeding profusely and she wrote underneath PJ's name 'forever'. There were drops of seawater in her eyebrows and her dark eyes glittered as she looked up at PJ.

'There you go – a sacred vow signed in blood by both of us. Marie-Claire Tierney and PJ forever.'

5

Black cat and kadaicha *boots*

PJ turned the corner into Kenneth Street, humming quietly to herself. Her socks squelched with seawater inside her school shoes and a white crust of salt was already forming on the brown leather. It wasn't until she turned into the driveway of her house that she started to worry about how to explain why her uniform was soaking wet.

All of a sudden, she missed Brian. She wanted to see his red Volkswagen Beetle parked in front of the house, smell the patchouli and Drum tobacco wafting out through his bedroom door. If he'd been at home, she could have told him everything, knowing he'd never dob her in. She opened the front door, trying to ignore the lightning strike of cracked glass.

Luckily, no one saw PJ slip into the house. She tiptoed into the bedroom she shared with Sue and quickly changed out of her wet things, bundling them into a soggy pile and shoving them under the bed. She'd worry about them later, when she could sneak into the laundry unnoticed.

Mum was sitting at the kitchen table, her head in her hands, a box of Bex on one side and a glass of sherry on the other. In front of her, pressed into a smooth white square, was a letter.

PJ looked over her mum's shoulder and saw Brian's name scrawled at the bottom. Underneath, in red ink, he'd written, 'Give my love to Sue and Bubs.'

'Bubs' was everyone's nickname for PJ. Just seeing he'd written that made her eyes prickle with tears.

'Mum?'

Mum didn't respond, as if she wasn't even aware that PJ was standing beside her. Mum folded the letter over and smoothed the paper with her fingertips.

'You alright, Mum?' PJ asked again, resting one hand tentatively on her mother's shoulder.

'I just need to have a little lie down before I fix tea,' said Mum in a voice heavy with weariness.

PJ slipped out the front door into the garden and stood on the flat green lawn, taking deep breaths and holding back tears. Over by the side fence, Dr Crusoe was watering the big wild mass of roses that spilt over from her garden into the McArdles'. For years, no one had lived in the house next door and the garden had become like a jungle. Dad had offered to help prune everything back after Dr Crusoe moved in a few months ago, but she'd laughed and said she liked it wild. She didn't even mow the lawns.

When Dr Crusoe spotted PJ, she beckoned her over.

'Young Miss McArdle, I've been hoping to catch you. I have a favour to ask of you or your sister,' said Dr Crusoe. Her voice was deep and husky, despite her small size. She had dark, deep-set eyes behind thick glasses. 'I dropped by earlier, but there didn't seem to be anyone at home.'

'Mum's not feeling well and Sue's hardly ever at home anyway.'

'Then I think you are exactly the person I need to speak to. Why don't you come into my house and we can discuss my proposition over a glass of lemon cordial?'

It was cool and dark inside Dr Crusoe's house and it took a moment for PJ's eyes to adjust. A musty odour of books and heavy furnishings permeated the air. PJ followed Dr Crusoe into the kitchen. A giant black cat leapt off the table and entwined itself around Dr Crusoe's legs, its long, thick tail swishing in the gloomy half-light. It looked up at PJ with huge green eyes and she took a step back.

'I didn't know that cat was yours,' said PJ. 'I thought it was a wild cat. Sue reckons it attacked her in the back lane one night.'

'I didn't know it was my cat either, until very recently. It seems our wild cat has adopted me. One night I woke up to find this enormous creature on the pillow beside me. Ever since, she's been in and out of my house as if she owns it. I've called her Friday.'

Dr Crusoe loaded up a tray with cold drinks and chocolate biscuits and carried it into the living room. Friday jumped up onto the couch beside Dr Crusoe and curled into a ball, her long black tail encircling her. PJ sat down in a big brown leather armchair while Dr Crusoe poured them each a glass of ice-cold cordial.

'I think Friday recognised a kindred spirit. You see, we're a couple of tired old battlers,' said Dr Crusoe, laughing.

PJ sucked chocolate from the tips of her fingers and looked around. Every wall of the living room was covered by dark wooden shields and huge masks, with spooky, staring eyes.

'Is that why you keep all those weapons?' she asked, pointing to an arrangement of long spears and a rough-hewn longbow alongside a quiver of brightly feathered arrows. 'Did you use them or something?'

'No, of course not. I try to heal people, not wound them.'

'Then how did you get all this stuff? Did you buy it?'

'Some of it. I worked with the Flying Doctors for some years. Most of the things in this room are from my time in Central Australia, or from time I spent in Bougainville, in New Guinea. Others are from when I was in South America or the Philippines.'

'Wow! Did you fly the planes and everything?' asked PJ, entranced.

'No, we had a pilot who flew us where we needed to go, but I do have a licence to fly light aeroplanes.'

PJ looked at her with amazement and then around at the display of shields and spears.

'You must be so brave. I'd get the heeby-jeebies just walking down the hall in the dark or coming into the living room at night with all those weapons and stuff.'

'I don't think you would. You get used to things when you live with them all the time. Like old Friday here,' said Dr Crusoe, reaching out to stroke the cat. 'Which leads me to my proposition.'

PJ sat forward in her chair.

'I'm going away for a few weeks, to the far north, to visit old friends, and I'm worried about Friday. I've grown very fond of her these past few weeks and would like to feel she'll still be here to welcome me when I return. Friday is a very independent creature, like me. She'll need to feel it's worth waiting for me. So what I propose is this. I will pay you fifty cents a day to come into my kitchen and feed Friday so she doesn't get too much in the habit of going elsewhere for sustenance.'

'Fifty cents a day! That's $3.50 a week. That's a lot of money just to feed a cat!'

'She's not an ordinary cat,' said Dr Crusoe, stroking Friday affectionately. Friday opened one eye and looked across at PJ, and all of a sudden PJ felt $3.50 wasn't so much money if it meant having to be in a dark empty house with this evil-looking creature.

'But how would I get in, and what if Friday didn't come when I called?' she asked.

'You don't need to worry about either of those things. I'll give you a key, and if you stand inside the back door and tap the side of Friday's bowl, she'll know you're here.'

Looking into Friday's huge green eyes, PJ got the feeling the black cat knew everything that was going on in the whole neighbourhood. One of its ears was frayed and torn and a pale scar arced across its face. PJ wriggled uncomfortably in her chair.

'Or perhaps you're not quite old enough for this sort of responsibility,' said Dr Crusoe, looking at PJ over the top of her glasses.

'No. I can do all that,' said PJ, quickly. Even if Friday was scary, she desperately wanted the job.

PJ looked away from the cat's unblinking gaze so she wouldn't lose her nerve and suddenly noticed a pair of round, dark objects mounted on the wall above the mantelpiece. They were like two birds' nests – intricate woven tangles of feathers, twigs and hair.

'What are they?' she asked.

'My favourite slippers,' replied Dr Crusoe, teasing.

'You wear them?'

'No, not really. They're *kadaicha* boots,' she said. 'In Central Australia the *kadaicha* man wears them to cover his tracks. Some stories tell that they help him fly just above the ground, or that he becomes invisible once he slips them on.'

'Who?'

'The *kadaicha* man. He's the medicine man of the tribe. A very clever man.'

'Like you. Like a doctor?'

'Something like that, but the *kadaicha* man is also a powerful magician.'

PJ stared at the slippers. The idea of a magic man skimming over the desert sent a shiver up her spine. 'I've never seen a black person, except on TV,' said PJ.

Dr Crusoe sighed and straightened her glasses. 'Well, I like to think that things will change for both you and my Aboriginal friends. You know, our souls are all the same colour, my dear. Perhaps, if we have a new government, there'll be a change for the better in this country.'

'I don't think I like things changing too fast,' said PJ moodily, remembering the night Brian had left home.

'Miss McArdle,' said Dr Crusoe, suddenly fierce, 'You can expect poison from standing water. Without movement, without change, there can be no growth. Terrible events have happened in this country and we need to promise ourselves and each other that things will change for the better.'

PJ blinked. No grown-up had ever spoken to her so seriously, as if she understood about the world and what was going on in it. She tried to think of something intelligent to say.

'I think I get it. Me and Marie-Claire did something like that. We signed our names in blood and swore loyalty forever.'

'Is Marie-Claire your sister?'

'No way! My sister Sue would never do something like that. Marie-Claire's just a friend.'

'Ah well, sometimes the friends we choose, or as with Friday, who choose us, sometimes friends can become like family.'

For a moment PJ had a vision of Marie-Claire as her sister, sharing a room with her, walking to school with her, and thinking up crazy and exciting things to do. It was such a startling idea that PJ laughed out loud.

'That sure would change things,' said PJ.

'We can all use a bit of change in our lives,' said Dr Crusoe.

6

Night of the party

That night PJ dreamt of the *kadaicha* boots. She was in a desert, skimming across the hot red ground with the magic boots on her feet and a long hunting stick in her hand. She knew she was hunting, but she wasn't sure what for. Around her, the desert was still, and somewhere voices were singing. All night she travelled across the red desert, searching. She woke and looked out at the summer morning, the neat green lawn and the blue sky. The world had shrunk back to its old shape and size, but somehow it seemed stranger than the world of her dreams and she couldn't figure out why.

PJ lay in bed and listened to the music that was pounding out from the living-room record player. Mum and Dad must have gone out to the bowls club, and Sue was taking advantage of it. Sue had once said that she and

PJ were 'bowls orphans' because their parents spent nearly every Saturday at the club, but PJ knew Sue loved having the house to herself. PJ found her in the kitchen dancing around the table in a pair of cut-off jeans and a bright red halter top.

When the phone rang, Sue ignored it, as usual. Answering the phone was PJ's job, even though it was never for her and nearly always for Sue.

A man on the other end coughed and then asked for 'Jane'. PJ knew better than to say no one of that name lived there. She ran down the hall.

'Are you Jane to anyone at the moment?' she asked.

'Gross me out. Why would I pick a name even more boring than the one I've got?'

'Well, there's a man on the phone looking for a Jane. I just thought it might be you, seeing as how that guy rang up looking for Angie and then you thumped me for telling him you didn't live here. What am I meant to say this time?'

'Tell him to rack off.'

PJ reluctantly picked up the telephone again and apologised for the fact that Jane didn't live there after all.

'If this is a wrong number, why did you have to check? Is this some kind of prank? Did Jane tell you to get rid of me?' said the man, growing more and more irritated as PJ tried to explain. In the end, she hung up on him.

She went back to the kitchen and sat on the table,

swinging her legs in time to the music and watching Sue dance.

'Haven't you got anything better to do than watch me, Bubs?' said Sue.

'I have tonight. Melinda Porter, she's having this party. Sort of end of Grade Six graduation thingo. And by the way, do you reckon you could call me PJ instead of Bubs? I mean, I turned twelve last month.'

Sue turned around and smiled. 'PJ. Cute. So you're growing up, eh? What are you going to wear to this wild party of yours then?'

'Jeans?' replied PJ.

Sue looked PJ up and down, resting one finger thoughtfully on her lips.

'If you really are growing up, then I think it's time to play dress-ups like a proper teenager,' Sue announced. She took PJ's hand and dragged her down the hall to their bedroom.

By midday the room was strewn with half of Sue's wardrobe – glittery halter tops, velvet hotpants, bright miniskirts, flowing cheesecloth dresses, tie-dyed shirts and an array of chunky platform shoes. Sue made PJ try on nearly every piece of clothing she owned, but nothing fitted PJ quite the way it did Sue.

Sue stuffed wads of tissues into a bra and adjusted the straps while PJ wobbled uneasily in platform sandals. Finally, Sue settled on a wine-red velvet mini with a swirling black pattern embossed on the fabric. Sue held

PJ's chin in her hands while she applied a thick line of kohl under her eyes.

'I don't know about all this,' said PJ, frowning into the mirror.

'You look fab,' said Sue.

'Yeah, but I don't look like me,' said PJ.

'D'you want to look like a red-headed Dennis the Menace forever?'

'My eyes are stinging.'

'You have to suffer for beauty's sake, baby,' said Sue, coming at PJ again with a tube of mascara.

PJ tottered towards the doorway to escape. As she passed Brian's bedroom, she saw her mother in there, arms folded across her chest, her face tight with misery.

'Mum!' said PJ. 'You're home already?'

Mum was gazing up at the big black-and-white poster of Che Guevara that Brian had above his bed. The room smelt of old incense and stale cigarette butts. Mum turned and did a double-take when she saw PJ teetering on the platform shoes.

'Pauline! What on earth are you playing at?'

PJ put one hand on the door frame and shifted uncomfortably from one foot to the other. 'I'm not *playing*. Melinda's having a party tonight so Sue's helping me find something to wear.'

'You look like a trollop.'

'A what?'

'Why don't you wear that nice party dress I made you

last summer? The one with the blue daisies.'

Sue had followed PJ down the hall and now stood with her hands on her hips, staring at their mother with disdain.

'Mum,' she said with a groan, 'you can't make her wear that daggy old crap. She's almost a teenager.'

Mum pulled shut the door to Brian's room. Her jaw had that tight, clenched look it got just before she lost her temper.

'Susan, she is still a little girl and I am her mother, not you, so I will be the one to decide what type of dress is appropriate for her to wear. I will not have her following your example of dressing like a harlot.'

'Mum, it's 1972! Just because we don't have all your hang-ups about sex, that doesn't mean we're sluts!'

'Susan!' shouted Mum, her face dark red with anger.

PJ looked from her sister to her mother in despair. She wanted to shout that she didn't feel sexy or even like a woman. She still felt like a kid.

'I don't even want to wear a dress,' she said, miserably kicking off the platform shoes. But neither Sue nor Mum heard her. The fight was on in earnest and all PJ could do to escape it was duck into the bathroom and lock the door behind her.

PJ was the only one in an old-fashioned party dress. The skirt was too long to be sexy and too short to be stylish. Her only consolation was that it was long enough to cover the scab on her knee. Nearly every girl was in a miniskirt of one sort or another. Melinda wore a tiny pink one and a white crocheted top. Jenny had made her miniskirt out of strips of coloured suede.

'Guess what!' said Jenny excitedly. 'Mum took me out shopping this morning and we bought my first training bra.'

'What for?' asked PJ.

Jenny rolled her eyes.

'You know, to get you ready for when you really need one. You have to get used to it some time!' said Jenny.

In the bathroom, Amanda Nelson, the only girl in Grade Six with cleavage, was showing everyone her new black push-up bra. Melinda and Jenny both slipped into the bathroom to investigate.

PJ stood next to the table of party food, putting Cheezels on the end of her fingers and then eating them off one by one. It was the first time anyone had thrown a mixed party. Nearly every girl from both the Grade Sixes was there, and a handful of boys, but the boys stood in a corner of the room, their hands in their pockets.

PJ found herself looking for Marie-Claire, even though she knew she wasn't invited. Marie-Claire would have thought up something fun to do so everyone wouldn't have to stand around feeling so bored and uncomfortable.

PJ wandered out to the kitchen with the empty Cheezels bowl. Melinda's parents were having their own party. Most of the adults were standing around a portable television, keeping track of the election results. They all had on T-shirts like Julie's with 'It's Time' emblazoned across their chests.

'Hello. You're Brian McArdle's little sister, aren't you?' said a tall, thin woman wearing a brown poncho and long white leather boots.

'Yes,' said PJ nervously.

'I just wanted to tell you that I think your brother is marvellous. Your mother should be very proud of him, the way he stood up for what he believes in.'

PJ looked at her feet. She couldn't help thinking about the look on Mum's face as she'd read Brian's letter from Pentridge prison. She didn't want someone else to tell her what her mother should have been feeling.

By the time she went back into the living room, all the kids had started to drift outside, their disembodied voices wafting through the dark garden. PJ stood by the sliding glass doors and watched as a couple of boys climbed onto the fence and threw kumquats at the girls. Scott Collins and Andrew Bradstone were trying to be more mature and had dragged Amanda Nelson and Jenny out to the woodshed, while Melinda and a group of girls stood guard for them outside the door, excited that at least someone was caught up in the throes of romance.

PJ stepped out through the screen door and a rotten kumquat hit her in the chest She was picking off the bits of orange pulp when Mr Porter put his head around the door with an excited expression on his face. His breath smelt of red wine as he shouted out into the dark garden.

'Hey, kids, the Labor Party has won the election! We've got ourselves a whole new government!'

'Daddy! No one's interested in all that rubbishy politics,' said Melinda dismissively. She had her arms folded across her chest and was looking sulky. The excitement of waiting for Jenny and Amanda to come out of the woodshed was wearing thin.

Mr Porter laughed and went back to the kitchen. Some of the adults were cheering and there was the noise of a champagne cork popping and then the clinking of glasses.

Amanda and Andrew came out of the woodshed holding hands, followed by Jenny and Scott. Scott smirked and snapped Jenny's bra strap as she walked away from him.

PJ gently stroked the cut on her finger. The skin was healing now, a tender pink line like an exclamation mark. All of a sudden, PJ desperately wanted to go home. She wanted to get out of the wretched party dress. She wanted the whole weekend to be over with. She couldn't wait for it to be Monday afternoon when she would be walking home with Marie-Claire.

7

Heart of courage

Marie-Claire and PJ walked home together every day. They never ran out of things to talk about. Some days they'd find they had walked right past the end of PJ's street and all the way down to the beach.

'Let's go back to your place,' said PJ as they stood at the crossing, trying to decide whether to go to the beach.

'No,' said Marie-Claire. 'Let's go to your place.'

'But we've been to my place twice this week.'

Marie-Claire frowned and looked out over the bay. 'I don't want to go back to my place. Your place is more interesting.'

'How can you think my place is more interesting when you've got stables and a pony and such groovy parents. My mum and dad . . . well, you know. They're like anyone's mum and dad.'

'You told me last time you'd take me to see those kaddy-waddy things.'

'You mean the *kadaicha* boots?'

'Yeah, those. They probably still have some magic left in them, that's why you dreamt you were flying in them. And I still haven't met that spooky cat you keep talking about. Maybe you just made it all up.' Marie-Claire raised one eyebrow and stared at PJ.

'I'd never lie to you,' said PJ, blushing.

Back at PJ's house, they had a couple of glasses of milk and some bread and jam and ate the last of Mum's fairy cakes. Dad's car pulled into the drive as PJ and Marie-Claire headed over to Dr Crusoe's. He hauled his toolbox out of the back of the station-wagon and waved. 'Where are you two off to?'

'We're just going over to Dr Crusoe's to feed the cat,' said PJ.

'That mad old bat. Tell her I'm still willing to take out those gum trees and cut back that jungle on our boundary if she'll let me.'

'Dad! You know she likes it the way it is. Anyway, she's still in Alice Springs,' said PJ, taking Marie-Claire's arm and hurrying her down the path.

'They'll get into the bloody drains if she doesn't get them out,' he shouted after them, but PJ and Marie-Claire were already through Dr Crusoe's front gate, in the shadow of the gums.

The roses around the back verandah had grown even

wilder in the past few weeks. The girls had to push the brambles away to reach the screen door.

'It's like a witch's house,' said Marie-Claire breathlessly.

'Dr Crusoe isn't witchy. She's really nice.'

PJ pushed her hand into the tangle of roses to one side of the back door, feeling for the loose brick that the key was hidden under. The hinges creaked as she pushed the door open and stepped into the sunroom. The house had a musty closed-up odour. PJ reached into the cupboard and pulled out a can of cat food.

'Bring me Friday's bowl, will you?' asked PJ.

'Why don't you call her first?' asked Marie-Claire.

''Cause she scratched me last time I went near her. I've worked out if I put the food in the bowl first and then stand clear, I won't get hurt.'

'She's only a cat,' said Marie-Claire. She stood at the back door holding Friday's empty bowl and banged it with a spoon. 'Here, puss!' she called.

From above them came a loud miaow. They both looked up, startled. Friday was sitting on top of a high cupboard staring down at them, her bright green eyes like magic orbs.

'Wow!' said Marie-Claire. 'I didn't see her come in. She's huge! That's no ordinary cat – that's a panther! Just like Bagheera in *The Jungle Book*!'

Friday leapt down from the cupboard and rubbed her long body against Marie-Claire's legs. Marie-Claire

45

scooped up the cat and staggered a little under the weight.

'I thought you said she was mean,' said Marie-Claire, nuzzling Friday's tattered ears with her chin.

'She's mean, to me,' replied PJ, grumpily scraping the food into Friday's bowl.

'I guess I'm like Mowgli, and the cat can see I'm kind of magic. Speaking of magic,' said Marie-Claire, lowering Friday to the floor, 'I want to see those magic shoes.'

PJ felt uncomfortable walking around in Dr Crusoe's place without her there. A niggling sense of guilt assailed her as she led Marie-Claire into the front of the house. It was so quiet, their footsteps echoed loudly on the wooden boards in the hallway. Marie-Claire seemed perfectly at home. She reached up and touched the tips of the spears on the wall and then took down a carved wooden mask from its hanging place and held it up to her face.

'Don't,' said PJ.

'It's okay. I know what I'm doing. I've read all about voodoo and witchcraft. This stuff can't hurt us.'

'It's not our stuff to muck around with,' said PJ.

In the living room, the *kadaicha* boots looked stranger than ever, as if they were walking straight up the wall above the mantelpiece. Marie-Claire reached up and pulled a tiny feather from one of them.

'Hey!' said PJ 'You shouldn't have done that.'

'It's for you,' said Marie-Claire, offering the feather to PJ. 'It will give you some of the magic and make Friday like you.'

Reluctantly, PJ took the feather and tucked it into the pocket of her jeans.

By the time they got back outside, long shadows were stretching across the tangled garden. Friday sat in a tree and watched them as PJ locked the door and put the key back into its hiding place. PJ looked up into the cat's luminous eyes and could feel the tiny magic feather in her pocket, as if it was burning like an ember. Marie-Claire followed her gaze.

'Hey, Friday's got the right idea. Let's shinny up that gum tree. We'll be able to see what's going on in everyone's back gardens.'

The smooth white bark was slippery between their knees as they scrambled for a hand-hold. Marie-Claire made it up to the lowest branch first and reached down to pull PJ up after her. They each found a fork in the upper branches of the gum. It was cooler up there, with a breeze from the bay wafting through the leaves. Marie-Claire wrapped her legs around the branch and lay back, staring up at the fading blue sky.

'This is perfect,' she said.

'Wow, I never realised, you can see for miles from up here,' said PJ. The breeze blew her hair away from her face. Beyond the tops of all the houses, the bay glowed in the late afternoon sunlight. Bands of gold stretched across the surface of the water and the You Yangs were a smudge on the far horizon. A dark ship was navigating its way out between the Heads.

PJ climbed one fork higher and looked down on Marie-Claire.

'Melinda and Jenny used to like climbing trees but now they reckon only boys climb trees. They're too mature.'

'I love climbing trees and I'm not a boy and I'm really mature.'

'Yeah, but you're different.'

'So are you.'

PJ laughed.

'Do you ever wish you'd been born a boy?' asked PJ, stretching out on the branch and putting her hands behind her head.

'Nope,' said Marie-Claire.

'But boys get to do anything they want and they don't have to wear dresses.'

'I still wouldn't want to be a boy. I'd never want to have to be a soldier.'

PJ felt that same rush of guilt she'd had by the railway line when Marie-Claire had talked about her dead brother.

'My dad says Gough Whitlam has stopped the draft and no one's gonna get conscripted anymore,' she offered hopefully.

Marie-Claire didn't say anything. She was staring out

to sea with a gloomy expression. PJ wanted to reach down and touch her but she picked a leaf instead and crushed it between her fingers, inhaling the lemony scent of the gum. The silence seemed to stretch on forever. Finally, PJ got up the courage to say something.

'Marie-Claire,' she said, gently, 'I'm really sorry about your brother.'

Marie-Claire glanced up at her. 'He was a hero. My brother was a hero. I went to Canberra with my mum and dad and they gave me all his medals – the Victoria Cross and a Purple Heart of Courage and heaps of other ones. There was a big parade and everyone was really proud of what he did and people threw flowers all over his coffin when we went out to the airport to get it because they knew my brother was a hero.'

'Wow! Did he save lots of people or something?'

Marie-Claire's eyes were bright and her cheeks flushed as she spoke. She wrapped her hands around the branch and spoke with a fierce intensity. 'He rescued all these little kids from this village who were caught in a minefield, and if they stepped on the mines, he slipped his bayonet underneath their feet and held down the trigger so it wouldn't blow up, and he guided them out of the minefield and they all got away and he saved them all, but then, right at the end, when he was saving the last person, his mate who was with him, the bayonet slipped and the mine went off and my brother was blown up and killed. But the other man, the one who stepped on the mine, he survived, even if his foot had got blown off, and he came back to Melbourne and he told us how my brother had saved him and everyone else – all those little kids would have died. He said my brother died a hero, a real hero.'

PJ felt her eyes brim with tears and she wiped them away with the back of her hand. Even if she never saw Brian again, at least she knew he was alive. She couldn't bear the thought of something like that happening to him. She climbed down onto the same branch as Marie-Claire and they sat together, watching the bay turn from blue to gold as the sun set behind the You Yangs.

It was dark by the time they walked into PJ's kitchen.

'Where have you been?' asked Mum crossly. 'I've had to set the table myself and tea's spoilt.'

'Sorry,' said PJ.

'It was all my fault, Mrs McArdle,' said Marie-Claire. 'We were having a really good chat and we lost track of time.'

Mum folded her arms and looked at Marie-Claire with narrowed eyes. 'I suppose your mother will be wondering where you are, young miss. Don't you think you'd better phone your parents and ask them to come and collect you?'

'We don't have a phone and anyway, it's not far. I'll walk.'

PJ stared at Marie-Claire. She *knew* Marie-Claire was lying – but why? She'd spoken to her on the phone heaps of times, and if her parents were so nice, they couldn't be cross about coming to get her.

'It's dark out there,' said Mum. 'I can't have you walking about at night all alone.' PJ could see she was irritated. 'Doug,' she called. 'Doug, can you drive this little girl home?' But as soon as Mum turned away, Marie-Claire ran out the back door, disappearing into the gathering dark.

8

The perils of Pauline

'Pauline, can you get the telephone?' called Mum.

PJ dashed into the hall and picked up the receiver.

'Bubs, it's me, Sue, but don't say anything. Say "Hello, Melinda" or pretend it's one of your other friends.'

'Oh yeah, hi, Melinda,' said PJ, glancing over her shoulder to check that Mum was still in the kitchen.

'Look, I have to ask you a favour,' said Sue. 'I can't come home. I'm round the corner, at the phone box outside the milk bar. If I come home, they'll never let me out the door. I want you to go to our room and get me my jeans – my Levis – and my silver platform boots and the black and green V-neck top, and meet me beside the railway line at five.'

'Why?'

'I'll explain when I see you. I can't tell you now. The olds will get suspicious. Just do it.'

'Okay, Melinda,' she said, feeling stiffly self-conscious, glancing down the hall to see if her mum was listening.

PJ felt a weird mix of excitement and apprehension as she gathered up her sister's clothes. She scoured the railway cutting in search of Sue and found her sitting in the long yellow grass smoking a cigarette, her school dress hitched up high, her legs stretched out in the late after-noon sun. PJ watched as she pulled on the skin-tight jeans.

'Oh God, what is this?' wailed Sue, running her hands up and down the denim.

'I ironed them for you. So that you'd look good.'

'You've put a crease in them, you dummy. Ironed jeans are so daggy! You didn't iron my undies as well, did you? You just don't do it, Bubs. Not Levis – you never iron Levis.'

'Sorry, I was trying to help.'

Sue sighed. 'Yeah, I know.' She licked her hands and rubbed the seamline flat with the palm of her hands.

'Where are you going?'

'I met this guy, at South Side Six, on Saturday night. He makes David Bowie look like a dag – he is *so* sexy. I'm meeting him at the TFM ballroom tonight. He's the lead guitarist in this band, Wolf, and he is such a spunk. I think he's falling for me.'

'But what will I tell Mum?'

'You won't tell her anything,' said Sue, rolling up her school uniform and cramming it into the bottom of her bag. 'You haven't even seen me, understand?'

Sue hitched her bag onto her shoulder.

'See ya, Bubs,' she called as she ran across the railway tracks. 'And thanks.'

Dad was in the front garden watering the azaleas when PJ turned into the driveway. She stood beside him, watching the sunlight shimmer on the arc of clear water.

'So what have you been up to, missy?' asked Dad.

'Nothing much.' PJ felt the blood rush to her cheeks. She quickly bent forward and let her hair fall across her face while she pretended to smell a flower. She didn't want Dad to notice her blushing.

'How's that little friend of yours, whatsername? The tall skinny one that's always hanging about these days.'

'Marie-Claire.'

'Funny name, that.'

'Not as funny as Pauline,' said PJ, standing up straight and pulling a face.

'You should be proud of being called Pauline. When I was a boy, I used to go to the pictures every Saturday and I loved it when they showed *The Perils of Pauline*. Tremendous stuntwoman, took your breath away.'

'Marie-Claire's mum used to be a stuntwoman sometimes, when she wasn't being an actress, and Marie-Claire used to do bareback riding for films too. When she was really little, before they moved to Melbourne.'

'Pull the other leg, love. It's got bells on it!' said Dad, chortling to himself.

'It's true!' said PJ, crossly, though somehow the story didn't sound quite as convincing as when Marie-Claire had first told it.

Dad reached out and took PJ's chin in his hand. 'Now don't you go believing every wild story you hear. That's how that brother of yours got himself caught up in all that mischief. You think for yourself, missy.'

He turned up the flow of the water and dragged the hose over to the hydrangeas. PJ watched him for a moment and then turned away. There was no point talking to Dad once he started on about Brian.

PJ let herself in through the back door and went straight to her bedroom. She didn't stop to talk to Mum and risk having to lie about Sue. She sat on the end of her bed and stared at the floor. The house was completely quiet. PJ picked at the chenille bedspread and wondered what it would be like to be an only child.

9

The secret tide

On the last day of school, PJ stood in the empty class-room after everyone had left and breathed in the stale smell of chalk and sweat and pencil shavings. She would never be in primary school again. She'd spent seven whole years in this place and now there'd never be a reason to come back. She ran her finger around the edge of her desk and wondered what the desks in high school would be like. Sue had told her a lot of gossip about high school, and PJ wasn't sure she liked the sound of it. She wished the holidays could last forever.

Marie-Claire was waiting at the gate for her.

'Maybe I could meet you at your place and we could ride our bikes down to the baths together,' said PJ as they walked away from the school. Everyone was meeting at the baths to celebrate.

Marie-Claire gave her a sidelong glance. 'No, I'll meet you at the baths.'

At home, PJ banged on the bathroom door and kicked at the steam curling up from under the door. Sue was in the shower.

'It's only me,' called PJ. 'I gotta get my bathers. I left them in there. Please, Sue. Everyone will be at the baths and I'll be the last one.'

PJ heard the bolt being drawn back and when she slipped into the steamy bathroom, Sue was already back in the shower.

'What are you doing?' asked PJ, staring at Sue, amazed.

'What does it look like? I'm dyeing my pubes.'

'Why?'

PJ stood clutching her bathers, watching with a mixture of fascination and revulsion. Black dye ran down Sue's legs and pooled in the bottom of the shower recess.

'Because they look better black. I hate them being blonde. No one has blonde hair and blonde pubes – not even Brigitte Bardot.'

'But you're a real blonde. Real blondes have blonde hair everywhere.'

'Weren't you on your way out?' said Sue, pulling the shower curtain across and turning her back on PJ.

PJ shrugged and slipped out of the bathroom.

At the Dendy Baths, the boys were doing bombs off the back wall, while the girls sat on the high weathered boardwalk, tanning themselves in the late afternoon sun. Marie-Claire grabbed PJ by the arm and pulled her over to the back wall, pointing at the long pier beside the baths.

'A man got eaten by a shark out there. Dived straight off the end of the pier and into his mouth.'

'Where do you get all these stories?'

'I listen, I hear things, that's all. My mother is a reporter, you know.'

'I thought you said she was an actress and a stunt-woman.'

'Yeah, well that was before. Now she's a reporter. So I hear a lot of stuff from her.'

PJ looked out across the bay at the tiny white sails that dotted the water, and the Heads, hazy in the late afternoon sun. Behind her, Scott Collins was doing bellyflops off the diving board and the smack of flesh on water resounded across the baths.

'Hey, Marie – you got an ironing board inside your bathers?' called Andrew Bradstone. Amanda Nelson giggled behind her hand. Marie-Claire looked bored.

'Let's get out of here,' she said, grabbing PJ by the arm. 'I'm sick of all this crapola.'

As they walked back along the boardwalk to the change rooms, they met Jenny and Melinda on their way to join the other kids.

'Where are you two going?' asked Melinda.

'We're leaving,' said Marie-Claire, walking straight past them.

'But we just got here,' said Jenny.

Guiltily, PJ stopped to talk.

'What's wrong with her?' asked Jenny, glaring at Marie-Claire's disappearing figure.

'There's nothing wrong with her,' said PJ. 'She thinks it's boring watching Scott Collins do bellyflops.'

'Is Scott here already?' asked Melinda, shading her eyes and looking excitedly towards the end of the baths.

'Who cares if he's here? Let's go catch up with Marie-Claire. We could all go down the beach together, the four of us. We could find some place just for us.'

'But this is the last day!' said Melinda. 'It's really exciting. We're almost teenagers. We don't want to play on the beach like little kids.'

'Besides, I don't want to hang out with that weirdo Marie-Claire,' said Jenny.

'She's not a weirdo,' said PJ crossly.

'Well, she's not our friend,' said Jenny.

'Yeah,' said Melinda. 'We've been your best friends since Prep. You should want to be with us, not her. We don't know why you're doing this, Pauline. She's just some dumb tomboy, and she's up herself too.'

PJ felt so angry she couldn't look at either of them. She glared down at the weathered boardwalk and the swelling sea beneath.

'Maybe I'm a dumb tomboy too,' she muttered, but they didn't hear her. When PJ looked up, they were already standing at the far end of the boardwalk watching Scott Collins spring off the high dive.

Marie-Claire and PJ walked along the sea wall, their thongs slapping loudly on the bluestones. They jumped off the sea wall into the shallows and walked arm in arm, kicking sprays of sand and seawater into the air, following the long ribbon of golden beach.

At the next stretch of beach, the air was heavy with the scent of coconut oil and tanning lotions. Teenage girls with long silky hair and tiny string bikinis lay on their stomachs, soaking up the afternoon sun. Sue was there, sitting on the steps of a bathing box smoking a cigarette, her head resting on the shoulder of a man with long dark hair. He was dressed in bright pink flares and a green and black striped shirt. He looked like a licorice allsort cast up on the beach, thought Pauline.

'That's my sister over there.' She nudged Marie-Claire.

'Do you want to go and say hello?'

'Not really. She doesn't like me talking to her when she's got a boyfriend around.'

'I'd be so stoked to have you as my sister, I'd introduce you to everyone,' said Marie-Claire, hooking her arm through PJ's. 'I wish we were twins and then we could do everything together.'

'We don't have to be sisters to be best friends,' said PJ, feeling giddy with happiness.

They walked on past the crowded beach and around

the point. There was no one on this last stretch of sandy beach before a rocky outcrop of reef but three dilapidated structures stood in a row at the far end of the beach. Two of them were little more than skeletons sticking up out of the sand, the weatherboards broken and stripped away. On the third, the black and green paint was peeling off the boards and the door was bolted shut. The tide was receding along the length of the beach but water still lapped around the stumps of the ruins as if the ocean was reluctant to let them go. Marie-Claire and PJ waded through the shallow water and sat on the steps of the black and green bathing box. No one from around the point could see them. It felt as if they owned this stretch of beach. They sat looking out to sea, towards Queens-cliff and Sorrento and the Heads, far away, etched sharp against the blue water and sky.

'One day we'll sail out through the Heads,' said Marie-Claire dreamily.

'When we grow up, we should go and live somewhere exotic and really far away, in a castle or something. We'll live somewhere so secret that not even our families will find us.'

'I'd want my family to find us. I'd like them to come and visit,' said PJ.

Marie-Claire didn't say anything. She traced a pattern in the sand on the step beside her.

'I wish my brother Brian would come home and visit us,' PJ said. 'I miss having him around. He used to argue with Dad some of the time, but now that he's not there Sue fights with Mum and Dad all the time, and it's much worse. She really screams at Mum. If Brian was there, he'd sort of calm everyone down.'

'My big brother used to be good like that too, but now he spends all day watching World Championship Wrestling and drinking beer and then he fights with my mum 'cause she worries about him and gets on his back. She never worries about me!'

'I thought your brother died in Vietnam.'

'I said my father, not my brother. You weren't listening. I think maybe my dad gets worn out from working at the hospital, saving lives and stuff. He's a doctor, you know.'

PJ felt that strange creeping feeling she had whenever Marie-Claire talked about her parents. Even though she talked about them a lot, PJ couldn't make a picture of them in her head.

'When are you going to ask me back to your place so I can meet your mum and dad?' said PJ. 'You've been to my place stacks of times.'

'You don't want to meet my family. What we need is our own place, so we don't have to go to each other's houses,' said Marie-Claire. 'Some sort of secret place that's only for us. Like a cave or a cubby or some place where it can be just the two of us.'

Suddenly, she turned around and pushed at the door of the bathing box until the timber creaked.

'What are you doing?'

'What does it look like?'

'Isn't this like breaking into someone else's place?'

'Nobody is looking after it. If no one looks after it, then it can't belong to anyone who deserves to own it.'

PJ had never been inside one of the bathing boxes before, but the glimpses she'd caught were of tidy little change rooms with bright towels hanging on the walls and piles of smart-looking beach gear. It was obvious no one had been in this one for years. There was an old table in the middle of the room with a bottle on it and little wind-drifts of sand were piled up in the corners. They could hear the sea lapping against the stumps beneath them. PJ felt a shiver of excitement. No one knew they were in here, with the door shut. There were no windows, but little chinks of light shone in through the cracks in the weatherboard and the pinholes in the rusty tin roof.

They pushed the door shut tight and lay on their bellies watching the tide through the cracks in the floor. The water swirled in circles, silvery green, sucking sand away from the stumps of the bathing box.

'I can't figure if the tide is going in or out,' said PJ, her face pressed against the cracks.

'That's because this is a secret tide,' said Marie-Claire. 'Like this is a secret place. The tide's especially coming right now 'cause we're inside. It's going to wash away the stumps and the whole bathing box is going to float out to sea on this secret tide. We'll sail right out – right out through the Heads and away from here. A long, long way, all the way around the world. And a magic albatross will come and sit on the roof and be our scout and watch over us. And we'll fall asleep and tomorrow we'll open the doors and there'll be nothing to see but the ocean in every direction.'

For a moment, PJ could see it exactly as Marie-Claire described it – the two of them, alone in the bathing box, sailing across a wide blue sea. She turned her head to look at Marie-Claire, but Marie-Claire was still watching the swirling waters beneath them.

'I'd like that,' said PJ.

'I'd love it,' said Marie-Claire fiercely.

10

Christmas blue

Every morning up to Christmas, Marie-Claire met PJ on the corner at the pedestrian crossing opposite the beach. Some mornings the footpath was so hot that they had to stand on their towels while they waited for the lights to change. The black tar was sticky underfoot as they hurried across Beach Road.

They always came with their beach bags crammed full of things. Marie-Claire brought a yellow candle, which she stuck in the empty wine bottle in the middle of the table, a stack of chipped crockery and an old folding chair. PJ always brought their lunch – Vegemite sandwiches, two Chocolate Royals, four slices of her Mum's homemade fruit cake and a thermos of cold lemon cordial. They put up Christmas decorations and even made a sort-of Christmas tree out of a piece of driftwood.

It was more fun decorating the driftwood tree in the bathing box than the Christmas tree at PJ's house. PJ had to drag the stepladder in and do the whole tree all by herself – even balancing the angel on the top. Every year up until this one, Dad had done the lights, Sue the tinsel, and Mum and PJ would tie all the glass ornaments in place. Brian always came home in time to fix the angel on the top. But this year, Sue was almost never at home, no one had heard from Brian since he'd got out of prison, and Mum always had a headache. Dad spent a lot of time watering the garden. He'd stay outside with the hose long after the dark had come down.

On Christmas Eve, PJ lay in bed and prayed harder than she ever had. Every other Christmas Eve she'd prayed for a pony, but this year she prayed that Brian would be there in the morning and they'd have the sort of Christmas they used to have.

It was the quietest Christmas lunch the McArdle family had sat through. PJ kept her fingers crossed, hoping that any moment Brian would walk in the door. Sue pushed the pudding around in her bowl, mashing the dried fruit against the side and fishing out the coins.

'I think I should move into Brian's old room,' she said.

'And where do you expect Brian to sleep?'

'Brian's not here anymore, if you haven't noticed. He's left this suburban hellhole for good!'

'Don't you talk about this home that way. Especially not in front of your baby sister!' said Dad, sharply.

'She's not a baby anymore, Dad. When are you going to wake up to what's happening around here? You're like a record stuck on the same boring track.'

'Just because Brian isn't here,' said Mum, 'just because he's made a mistake, it doesn't mean he's not part of this family.'

'Seems like he prefers Julie's family to ours as he's spending Christmas with them,' said Sue. 'I don't blame him. At least her family doesn't crap on about sex being sinful and father knows best and all that bullshit about having to do what you're told all the time. No bloody wonder that he doesn't want to be here.'

'Mind your *language*, Susan!' said Mum. 'And let me tell you, miss, just because Brian has been led astray by that girl, doesn't mean he's not the same good-hearted boy underneath.'

'That's pathetic. It's got nothing to do with Julie. You can't believe he's not your golden boy anymore, can you? You never think about me and Bubs – it's always Brian, isn't it? Brian this and Brian that – Brian, Brian, Brian all the bloody time. What about me?' shrieked Sue. 'You keep his room as if he's going to walk in the door tonight, while me and Bubs are squashed up together in that tiny back room. Why don't you wake up! Brian's nearly twenty-one, and he's *not coming back*!'

Sue pushed her chair out from the table and stormed out of the room. Mum followed her into the kitchen and the argument rose to angry screams. PJ looked at Dad, willing him to intervene, but he seemed really interested in a small smudge of custard that had fallen onto his shirt and was wiping at it with his serviette.

PJ put her hands over her ears and stared miserably at her half-eaten bowl of Christmas pudding.

That night, when Sue came into the bedroom, PJ turned over and pretended to be asleep. She didn't want to acknowledge the fact that Sue had pulled her schoolbag out from under the bed and was stuffing it full of clothes.

Finally, curiosity got the better of her.

'What are you doing?' she whispered.

'What does it look like?' said Sue.

There was a tapping at the door and Sue pushed the bag out of sight and leapt into bed, pulling the sheets up tightly around her neck. She glared across at PJ. 'Don't say a word.'

Dad put his head around the door.

'Don't let what your mum said get to you, possum. She's upset,' he said. 'She didn't mean it.'

Sue said nothing and Dad quietly pulled the door to.

As soon as his footsteps had faded away, Sue threw off the sheets and pulled her bag out again. PJ sat up in bed.

'What are you going to do?'

'There's a big rock festival up on the border over New Year. And then there's Sunbury after that. I didn't go last year, and I'm not missing it again just because they want to squash me into being as boring as they are. I'll bum a lift with someone, or hitch or something.'

'But have you got enough money to get in?'

'I'll be alright. I'll climb the fence. Stop thinking up things to put me off. You're as bad as Dad and Mum.' She was silent for a moment, then she said bitterly, 'Mum thinks I'm a real slut.'

'She wouldn't say that about you!'

Sue snorted and PJ realised she was crying. 'She said I was a Jezebel – it's the same thing in her book. It's what she calls Julie. She must hate me.'

'No she doesn't,' said PJ.

'You don't understand any of this, Bubs.'

PJ desperately wanted to think of something comforting to say, but Sue got up and slid the bedroom window open.

'You're coming back, after the festival, aren't you?' asked PJ, watching her sister straddling the windowsill, one leg in the bedroom and the other in the garden.

'I don't know,' said Sue.

'But what about when school starts? You have to come back for that.'

'I don't know what's going to happen. I don't feel like a schoolgirl anymore.' She jumped into the garden.

'Sue, wait,' said PJ as Sue began to slide the window down again.

PJ scrambled out of bed and snatched her piggy bank from the shelf. She pulled the rubber seal off the bottom and shook out all the coins she'd saved from the Christmas pudding and summer jobs. 'Here, you might need this,' she said, thrusting the handful of coins and dollar bills into her sister's hand.

Sue leant back through the window and kissed PJ on the cheek. She smelt warm and smoky and her long blonde hair was bright in the moonlight.

'Thanks, Bubs. You're a good kid,' she said.

And then she was gone.

PJ climbed back into bed. It gave her the creeps to be in the room all alone with Sue's empty bed staring at her. She wanted to hear the sound of Sue's breathing from across the room, the sound of someone close to her. She shut her eyes and curled into a small tight ball, thinking of the bathing box and the secret tide that would sweep her and Marie-Claire out into the blue ocean.

11

The visiting game

Marie-Claire and PJ spent the whole of Boxing Day afternoon at the beach. PJ had to keep a T-shirt on – her skin was already raw and red with sunburn. Marie-Claire had a smudge of zinc across her nose but otherwise she was golden-brown all over. When the tide came in, they lay on their stomachs in the bathing box and watched the sea swirling under the floorboards.

'We could be anywhere, couldn't we?' said Marie-Claire dreamily.

'What do you mean?' asked PJ.

'Well, we could be in the South of France, you know, on the Riviera in our own private chateau.'

PJ looked around at the grey weatherboards and laughed.

Suddenly, Marie-Claire sat up. 'No, really. Don't you ever do that? When you're in some place, you imagine it's

71

somewhere else, or that you're someone else?'

PJ shrugged. It was such a Marie-Claire thing to say. She looked at the world in a way that made PJ feel short-sighted.

'Sometimes I imagine that my brother Brian has come home.'

'That's not what I mean.'

'Don't you ever wish your brother was still alive?'

Marie-Claire didn't answer. She rolled back onto her stomach and pressed her face against the cracks in the floor.

The afternoon shadows were long across the suburban gardens by the time they walked up from the beach.

'That house – I could imagine living in that place, there. I'd like a house like that, one day,' said Marie-Claire.

PJ looked at the old mansion. It had gargoyles and orange tiles on its roof, the garden was full of giant oak trees, and there was a big enclosed verandah running along the front of the house.

'My dad knows those people,' she said. 'He's done jobs for them – done their drains and then replaced all their locks when they got burgled last year. That's the McGregors' house. I reckon they're really rich. They've got a beach house down at Rosebud too.'

'Are they there now? Down at Rosebud?' asked Marie-Claire, her face alive with interest.

'I don't know. Why?' asked PJ.

'I'd like to see inside.'

'We can't. They're not at home.'

Marie-Claire raised one eyebrow and grinned, her teeth very white against her sun-browned face.

'See up there,' she said, pointing, 'that little window on the second floor. I betcha that's open. Those sort of windows never get locked. We could shinny up the stinkpole and be in there in a couple of minutes.'

'I don't . . .'

'What's the matter with you, PJ? It's not like we're going to take anything. We're just going to check on the place.'

'What if we get sprung?'

'Don't be a scaredy-cat,' said Marie-Claire, as she walked in through the front gate and hid her beach bag under a bush behind the front fence. 'C'mon.'

Before PJ could object, Marie-Claire was running across the front lawn. The afternoon sunlight flashed through the leaves, dappling her body as she ran.

PJ stood in the driveway, looking from the street to the house. She knew that what Marie-Claire was doing was wrong but she couldn't let her do it all alone. Sighing, she jogged over to where Marie-Claire was standing among the hydrangeas, her hands curled around the stinkpole.

Marie-Claire was like a monkey. In less than a minute she'd reached the small window and hoisted it open.

'See,' she hissed over her shoulder before sliding

across the sill head-first. The last thing to disappear from sight was her thongs.

Getting in through the tiny window was a tight squeeze for PJ. It opened into a small toilet with pale green walls. Marie-Claire watched as PJ slid over the sill and landed on her hands on the floor.

'We shouldn't be doing this,' said PJ as she got to her feet. The paint from the pole had left chalky white marks on the inside of her legs and she dusted it off.

'You don't mind going inside Dr Crusoe's house when she's not there.'

'That's different. She asked me to do that.'

'Relax,' said Marie-Claire impatiently. 'This is just us being like sort of spirits – good spirits, like brownies. I mean, we're not gonna take anything or break anything. We're gonna imagine what it must be like to be the people who live here. Imagination – that's a good thing to use. We're not doing anything wrong so long as we don't touch anything.'

PJ wasn't so sure. Her heart was racing – she was sure someone was going to spring them. She'd never been inside the McGregors' house. It was even bigger on the inside than it looked from outside. The hallway was panelled with dark wood and there was a long stair-case with a shiny wooden banister. Marie-Claire slid down it, her damp bathers squeaking on the slippery polish, her thighs turning pink from the friction. PJ stared at her as she stood at the foot of the sweeping staircase rubbing her legs, willing her to want to leave.

'Next time, we'll have dry bums and slide down the banister heaps,' called Marie-Claire.

'I don't know about next time,' PJ said as she padded down the stairs, her bare feet sinking into the thick, soft carpet. She traced her finger along the edge of a white marble table at the foot of the stairs. It was so cold to touch that she shivered.

Marie-Claire had already crossed into the living room and flung herself onto a huge floral sofa piled high with embroidered cushions. PJ could see her reflected in the giant golden-framed mirror that hung above the mantel-piece.

'This is the sort of room I might have when I'm rich,' said Marie-Claire, sinking back among the cushions.

'I thought you were going to have a swanky apartment in Paris or a treehouse in some African jungle.'

'Yeah, well I'll have a place like this in Melbourne, for when I come back to visit you.'

'And I thought I was coming with you,' said PJ darkly.

'Don't worry about it. Come and feel how bouncy this couch is.'

PJ didn't want to bounce on the couch. Marie-Claire was already making damp marks on the upholstery. She knelt down on the floor beside the couch and looked up at Marie-Claire. As hard as PJ fought it, she couldn't help feeling a little shimmer of guilty excitement.

Marie-Claire lay back and put her hands behind her head. 'Look at that chandelier up there. It makes you think, doesn't it? There's a line from this poem, *The world is so full of a number of things, I'm sure we should all be as happy as kings*. That's Robert Louis Stevenson, and I reckon he's right. You look at something like that chandelier and you have to think how amazing the world is.'

PJ lay back on the carpet and stared up at the glittering cut-glass chandelier. A shaft of late afternoon sunlight shone through the crystals and sent a pattern of rainbows stretching across the ceiling. Staring up at the swirling colour and light, PJ felt she and Marie-Claire weren't in someone else's house, they were in another world together. For a moment, PJ could imagine it really was their home and she and Marie-Claire really did own the mansion.

It felt as though they'd been inside the McGregors' house for hours before PJ finally persuaded Marie-Claire to leave. They slid back down the stinkpole outside the upstairs bathroom window. Marie-Claire dusted off her hands as she stood in the hydrangeas.

'See,' she said. 'That was really fun. I'm gonna carry that around inside my head, the picture of us being in that house. 'Cause one day we're going to live somewhere even fancier than that.'

That night as PJ lay alone in the dark of her quiet room, the picture of herself and Marie-Claire standing in front of the gilt mirror, laughing, kept coming back to her – the two of them in that big shining mirror. She tried to imagine them together somewhere, far away from their families, just the two of them.

It was so different being friends with Marie-Claire. She wasn't like anyone PJ had ever known before. She made PJ feel like anything could happen, as if life was something that you just invented as you went along and none of the old rules mattered. It was scary and exciting in the same instant. Lying in the quiet dark, PJ crossed her fingers and wished as hard as she could that the feeling would last forever.

12

Being Marie-Claire

The house felt like a morgue, it was so empty. Mum and Dad had gone off to play bowls, and for a minute PJ could imagine what it would be like to be an orphan. She walked from room to room, running her finger across the top of the furniture, checking for dust. There was nothing else to do. It was so hot. She lay on the floor in the hallway, the carpet prickly beneath her bare legs and stared at the ceiling, waiting for Marie-Claire. A daddy-long-legs was spinning a small web in a corner as she waited.

Marie-Claire wanted to look at everything, going through Sue's things, messing around in cupboards and drawers, as if there was something interesting to find in every corner. When she skipped into Brian's room, PJ started to feel uncomfortable.

'We shouldn't be in here. There's nothing that would be interesting to you.'

Marie-Claire ignored her and pulled a box of records out from under Brian's bed.

'Hey, I love this song. It's about me. It's about being Marie-Claire. Come on.'

In the living room she put the record on the player. PJ tried to make out what the singer was saying while Marie-Claire danced around the furniture, miming the song:

But where do you go to my lovely . . . when you're alone in your bed.
Tell me the thoughts that surround you. I want to look inside your head.

'Yuk, sounds like he's a brain surgeon or something,' said PJ.

Marie-Claire stopped dancing. 'You have no sense of romance. This is a really romantic song, Pauline McArdle.'

'Don't call me Pauline. My name is PJ.'

'Well, stop acting like a Pauline.'

PJ tried not to sulk. 'We should put the record back. If Brian comes back and finds I've been going through his stuff, he'll go berko.'

'I thought you said he'd left home.'

'Well, that doesn't mean he won't come back for his stuff, one day.' PJ felt a stab of doubt even as she spoke. It was nearly two months since she'd seen Brian.

'I'm not going to break it or anything. I'm just going

to play it. It's my favourite and he can't be very interested in it anymore or he'd come and get it. Listen, I love this bit – about all the places in France that I go to,' she said. She clenched her fist as if she were holding a microphone and mimed the lyrics:

And when the snow falls you're found in St Moritz
With the others of the jet set
And you sip your Napoleon brandy
But you never get your lips wet.

'It's not about you. It doesn't even sound like something you'd do,' said PJ.

'It could be. I'll be like that one day. You'll see. I'll have holidays in France and all that stuff.'

'And a topless swimsuit?' asked PJ.

'Maybe,' said Marie-Claire. 'But I'll do all those things the other Marie-Claire does.'

She danced around the living room some more and then spotted the silver tray that PJ's mum kept on the sideboard with a half-empty bottle of sherry on it.

'Hey, why don't we practise!' she said, grabbing the bottle and waving it at PJ. 'Let's sip a Napoleon brandy, but never get our lips wet.'

'No way,' said PJ. 'I'll get in big trouble.'

'We won't drink that much of it. It means you're really classy, if you can drink Napoleon brandy and not get your lips wet.'

'But this isn't brandy, it's sherry. It's probably the stuff Mum uses in the trifle.'

'Let's try it anyway,' said Marie-Claire, her eyes bright. PJ felt a flutter of alarm in the pit of her stomach. It was a feeling she was getting used to. It was part of being friends with Marie-Claire.

Marie-Claire tipped her head back, opened her mouth to pour the sherry in and swallowed hard. Tears sprang to her eyes and she spluttered and laughed.

'That didn't look very classy,' said PJ, laughing. 'And your lips *are* wet. Matter of fact, you look like you've been drooling.'

Marie-Claire grinned and dropped the bottle into PJ's lap.

'You try it then.'

PJ curled her fingers around the neck of the bottle and tipped her head back. Somehow she managed to keep her throat open and let the burning liquid flow down.

'Wow,' said Marie-Claire, admiringly.

PJ smacked her perfectly dry lips. 'Did it look classy?'

'Well, not really – you looked a bit spazzo, but it was sort of impressive.'

PJ giggled. Her chest felt hot and tight. Suddenly she looked at the bottle and felt a wave of panic. What would her mum say when she realised someone had been drinking the sherry? Once upon a time she would have blamed Sue, but now there was no one to blame except PJ.

'I hate being an only child,' she said suddenly.

'I wish I *was* an only child,' said Marie-Claire. 'I mean, even though my brother's dead, it's like he's still around,' she added, quickly. 'It's like all Mum and Dad think about is Kevin and never me. It's like they never see me.'

'My mum and dad see everything I do. When Sue and Brian were around, I thought I hated being invisible. But now it's really freaky – there's no one but me at the table and we don't even sit in the dining room anymore. Mum says there's no point now that it's just the three of us, so we eat in the kitchen and no one says anything. I feel like I should do all the talking, but I'm not used to it. I don't know what to say. Even if everyone argued a lot when Brian and Sue were here, at least things got said. The quiet is creepy.'

'So what's happened to your brother and sister?'

'I don't know. Mum reckons Brian is "living in sin" with Julie, so we're not allowed to see them. And Mum doesn't want me to see Sue either. She reckons she's a bad influence. So it's just me now, and it's kind of lonely. At least you've got all those animals at your place.'

'You've got Friday,' said Marie-Claire.

'Friday is Dr Crusoe's cat, not mine. Your place sounds a whole lot more interesting than my place. Everything in my house is boring.'

'I don't think so,' said Marie-Claire. 'You're not boring.'

'Are you trying to fob me off again?' asked PJ.

Marie-Claire didn't answer. The song came to an end

and Marie-Claire jumped up and started the record again. Above the sideboard was a small square mirror. Marie-Claire stood in front of it and pressed her lips against the glass.

'*Your loveliness goes on and on, yes it does,*' she sang to her reflection. 'Let's not crap on about our families and our houses and all that stuff. Let's do something interesting. Let's practise kissing.'

'Why?'

'Well, have you kissed a lot of guys?'

'No.'

'Then how are you going to know if they're doing it right, or that you're any good to kiss, if you don't practise it first?'

PJ was feeling a little sick from the sherry. 'I'm not in a hurry to kiss anyone.'

'PJ, don't be a baby!'

'We could kiss a doll or something,' she suggested feebly.

'A doll can't tell you if you're doing it right!' said Marie-Claire seriously.

'Okay, then what?'

'We'll practise on each other,' said Marie-Claire decisively, staring at her own reflection. PJ pulled a face and shrugged in resignation.

It felt so weird having Marie-Claire's face next to her own. She could see the smooth honey-coloured skin, with a small line of darkened pores on the edge of her nose. PJ shut her eyes and tried to imagine she was kissing a boy.

She pressed her lips against Marie-Claire's. She could smell the sherry on their breath. 'Where Do You Go To, My Lovely?' was playing in the background again.

Suddenly, Marie-Claire pulled away. 'You're not doing it right. You're meant to use your tongue.'

'Like how?' asked PJ, disgusted at the thought.

'You have to put your tongue in my mouth. That's what you do when you French-kiss.'

'Yuk!'

'Forget it,' said Marie-Claire, sighing. 'Let's go to the beach. We can have some lunch in our bathing box.'

PJ nodded. At the bathing box, they wouldn't have to worry about their families or kissing boys. At the bathing box they could be themselves.

13

Burning bras, burning bridges

PJ lay sprawled on the living-room floor, shaving the
ends off her pencils and writing her name on the clean
piece of wood. She loved the way all the new stuff smelt,
the tang of the wooden pencils, the cellophane and
plastic and new wrappings. But when she thought of
being in high school she found herself wishing Sue and
Brian were around to admire her in her school uniform,
looking so much older. She remembered the time they'd
come and watched her at the end of kindergarten
when she'd been an angel in the Nativity play. They'd
been much bigger than everyone else's brother and
sister, she'd been so proud. She missed them so much
it hurt.

Mum drove her to school on the first day. She stared
out the window at the gangs of kids walking to school and
felt embarrassed.

'I should have ridden my bike,' she said, squirming in her seat.

'It's your first day,' said Mum. 'I'll pick you up too. I want to take you shopping for a bra.'

'A bra! I don't want a bra!'

'You've put on a bit of puppy fat this summer, Pauline. Now you're in high school, you don't want to leave getting a bra until everyone notices you need one.'

'I don't need a bra and I can catch the bus home,' said PJ, quiet desperation in her voice.

'Nonsense, you don't even know where the bus stop is.'

'Marie-Claire will.'

Mum frowned.

'I'll be waiting outside the front gate at 3.30,' she said.

Outside the school, PJ joined the hundreds of kids streaming in through the gate. She passed tough-looking boys with cigarettes tucked into their T-shirt sleeves, smoking surreptitiously beneath a stairwell. The air around them was tangy with the scent of tobacco. There were sharpies with crew cuts and stringy rats-tails dangling over their shirt collars, and skinheads with their hair cropped so close you could see their scalps. She tried not to stare.

Inside, she passed through long, cool corridors lined with grey metal lockers. Marie-Claire was sitting up the back of the classroom, waiting for PJ. Her school blazer was too big for her. Melinda and Jenny were sitting in the very front desk. They turned and stared at

PJ disapprovingly as she slipped into the desk beside Marie-Claire.

At lunchtime, PJ and Marie-Claire sat on the edge of the netball court with dozens of other new kids. Melinda and Jenny were there too, but they didn't speak to PJ and Marie-Claire. They were busy talking to some prissy-looking girls who'd come from Wilson Street Primary. One of them pulled a copy of the new *Cleo* magazine out of her schoolbag and the girls fell about laughing with embarrassment at the centrefold. PJ tugged on Marie-Claire's blazer sleeve and then got up and walked away, expecting Marie-Claire to follow her, but Marie-Claire stayed sitting among the other girls, her long legs stretched out in front of her. PJ stomped back and stood in front of Marie-Claire, glaring down at her.

'C'mon. Let's go,' she said.

'Go where?' asked Marie-Claire.

'I don't know. Just somewhere.'

Marie-Claire shrugged. 'If you don't know where you want to go, we may as well sit here,' said Marie-Claire. 'I want to hear the gossip.'

Resentfully, PJ sat back down on the bitumen beside Marie-Claire. The thought of having to spend every lunchtime sitting around with all these girls, talking about boys and clothes and nail polish, made her feel numb with boredom. She wished the summer holidays hadn't come to an end so quickly.

PJ slumped low in her seat as her mum drove away from the school gate. Marie-Claire had headed off to catch the bus with a whole gang of new kids. PJ felt like the only kid in the whole school who was getting a lift home.

They stopped in the shopping centre and parked near Anna-Louise's Paris Lingerie shop. PJ dragged her feet all the way, trying to think how she could talk her mother out of buying her a bra. Suddenly, Mum grabbed PJ's arm and dragged her into the chemist. She bobbed down behind a shelf laden with sunglasses and deodorants.

'What is it, Mum? What's wrong?'

'It's your sister. She's out there.'

PJ peered over the top of the shelving, hoping to catch sight of Sue, but Mum pulled her back down.

'Why don't we go out and say hello? Why are we hiding?'

Mum looked exasperated and squeezed PJ's arm even tighter.

'Didn't you see?' she said under her breath, as much to herself as to PJ. 'She looks like a clown, or worse – like a prost—' She looked away from PJ and shut her eyes. PJ had always thought of her mum as being brave and strong, but at that moment, with the corners of her mouth turned down and her lip trembling, she looked like a little girl. It was so strange to see her hiding beside a shelf of talcum powder, one hand shielding her face.

PJ peered out from behind the deodorant bottles. Sue wore long silver boots with chunky platform heels, a pair of red velvet hotpants and a tight black T-shirt. She was smoking a cigarette, watching the traffic. PJ saw an old Holden pull up at the kerb with a long-haired man behind the wheel. Sue leaned in through the window, laughing, and then, instead of opening the door, she slid right in through the open window. The Holden drove off.

That night in the kitchen, Mum and Dad were morose. Mum had hardly said a word since the incident in the shopping centre. She seemed to forget why they'd gone shopping in the first place, and took PJ home without even mentioning the bra. She'd spent the rest of the afternoon sitting on the couch in the living room, turning the pages of an old photo album full of baby photos and touching the pictures, almost as if she could feel the soft skin of their faces.

PJ ate her sausages and mashed potato as fast as she could, mixing the peas in with the mash and wolfing it down. She couldn't wait to get away from the table. She hurried out of the kitchen and into the warm summery evening. It was still light outside and cicadas were singing in every corner of the garden.

Three ripe apples dropped into the grass as PJ swung into the apple tree. Usually PJ felt completely invisible among the fruit and leaves, but tonight she knew that someone was watching her. She pushed back a branch and looked out. Friday was sitting on the fence, only a few feet away. The big black cat's eyes seemed to look right through PJ's skin. Suddenly, the sound of Dr Crusoe banging on Friday's bowl resounded in the still evening air. Friday leapt down off the fence and ran into the tangled jungle that was Dr Crusoe's garden. PJ stepped from the tree onto the fence and followed her.

It was cool inside Dr Crusoe's kitchen. Dr Crusoe mixed them both a spider with green lemonade and vanilla ice-cream. PJ propped her elbows on either side of the glass and licked the froth from the top.

'Friday has been having a bad influence on you. You look exactly like a cat when you do that – a tabby, I think.'

PJ smiled. 'I think Friday's glad you're back. I don't think she really liked me.'

'Friday is a deep thinker. Most cats decide who they love or hate very quickly, but Friday's a watcher. She takes her time. I think she watched me for quite a while before she decided we belonged together.'

'She liked my friend Marie-Claire straight away,' said PJ.

'Perhaps Friday could see straight through her. Perhaps she could see that Marie-Claire needed her. Whereas you might have a lot more layers, so Friday hasn't quite worked you out. You're probably more interesting to Friday.'

'I think it's the other way round,' said PJ. 'Marie-Claire's a lot more interesting than I am. We both started high school today and she said our whole lives are going to change. She thinks we have to act more grown-up or something but I'm not so sure.'

'A rite of passage!' said Dr Crusoe, smiling. 'I've always thought we don't do enough to mark this sort of occasion. The tribal people I've worked with have very clear ideas about how a young man or a young woman should be initiated into their tribe. This calls for us to open a packet of Tim Tams in honour of your big day.'

PJ grinned. 'Mum wanted to buy me a bra in honour of my big day. I think I'd rather have a packet of Tim Tams any day.'

They took their spiders and the Tim Tams into the front of the house, and sat on the enclosed verandah in a pair of big cane armchairs padded with soft green velvet cushions, and watched the garden grow dark.

'It's a funny thing about the way we whitefellows live. All these young hippies didn't get a proper initiation, so they've had to invent it for themselves. My generation, we had the Great Depression and the war to shape us. But these young ones have been swept out to sea on the tide of growing up.'

'I don't think I want to grow up,' said PJ. 'Not if it means having to wear bras and sit around listening to boring gossip and never doing anything interesting. My brother's girlfriend, Julie, she burnt her bra at a rally. My mum thought that was shocking, and I thought it was dumb, but now I'm not so sure. I'm not so sure about a lot of things anymore.'

'Growing older is a great adventure, PJ, and having doubts along the way is very natural. Everything changes.'

PJ took another Tim Tam.

'At least there's one thing I can be sure of. I'll always love chocolate biscuits, no matter what.'

It was pitch dark by the time PJ swung herself over the fence into her own garden. She was just about to push the swing door into the kitchen when she heard someone crying on the other side. She stopped, her hand in mid-air. It was the scariest sound she'd ever heard. She'd never known Mum to cry, ever.

'Now, love,' murmured Dad in a low voice. 'Settle down. She hasn't burnt all her bridges yet. She'll come back to us when she's ready.'

'But Doug, can't you see we've lost her,' cried Mum, her voice jagged with grief.

PJ nearly burst into the kitchen to reassure them she wasn't lost at all, but suddenly she realised they weren't talking about her. They were talking about Sue.

PJ went to her room and sat on Sue's old bed and thought about what she'd overheard. She didn't feel Sue was completely lost – more adrift, floating away from the family and off into a whole different world. All of a sudden, PJ could imagine everyone in the family – Brian, Sue, her mum and dad – on separate rafts, floating away from each other on different currents, being swept out to sea.

14

Looking for trouble

Miss Dickers, the vice-principal, stood at the double doors of the auditorium, waiting. She was a short, angry-looking woman in a bottle-green outfit. On either side of her were a pair of Form 6 prefects. One of them was holding a plastic box. As the long queue of girls shuffled past, the vice-principal tapped anyone wearing jewellery with her ruler.

'No jewellery allowed,' she said to Marie-Claire. 'Take that chain off and you can collect it at the end of the school day.'

'I can't take it off. My godmother had the chain soldered shut when I was seven. It's a special sort of ritual my family has.'

'Nonsense. Are you looking for trouble, young lady? Take it off at once.'

'I can't.'

Miss Dickers reached up and her hand closed around the gold chain. With one swift movement, she tore it from Marie-Claire's neck. PJ heard Marie-Claire's sharp intake of breath. She felt an answering stab of outrage as Miss Dickers dropped the chain into the plastic box.

'You can come and collect it at 3.30. There are no exceptions to the jewellery rule.'

They sat at the back of the auditorium. Marie-Claire had one hand on her collarbone, where the gold chain had been.

'I hate that woman,' she said in a low, angry voice.

'Did your godmother really solder the chain on?'

'She might have. Miss Dickface doesn't know otherwise.'

PJ wished Marie-Claire had taken off the chain when Miss Dickers had asked. From then on, every time they had to walk past her office, PJ could feel her heart beating faster. She had a feeling the vice-principal wouldn't forget Marie-Claire's refusal to co-operate, and she wasn't wrong. The next day, Marie-Claire and PJ were stopped in the corridor.

'You two,' called Miss Dickers. 'My office. Right now.'

'She's got it in for me now,' whispered Marie-Claire.

In the office a line of girls were kneeling on the floor. PJ and Marie-Claire stared questioningly at Miss Dickers.

'Uniform check,' said Miss Dickers and pointed them to the end of the row.

They all knelt in silence while Miss Dickers walked the length of the row with a yardstick, measuring the distance between the hem of the dress and their knees. PJ felt the back of her neck prickle with sweat. If there was more than six inches between her knees and the hem of her skirt, she'd score two detentions and Miss Dickers would make her unpick the hem straight away. She'd have to spend the rest of the day walking around the school with a ragged hem.

Tracy Grogan was kneeling at the end of the line-up. Miss Dickers took her chin in her hand and tipped her head upwards. Tracy's long blonde hair fell away from her face and she stared up at the vice-principal. She was so thin she could have passed for ten years old, with her skinny legs and stick-like arms. She had a little scar above her left eye, and her pale blue eyes were rimmed with thick black eyeliner. It made her expression look fierce and defiant.

'This is the third and last time I'm going to talk to you about wearing make-up to school, Tracy.'

Miss Dickers crossed to her desk and took a bottle of make-up remover from her drawer and a box of Kleenex.

'You're not leaving this office until every last skerrick has been removed.'

Black mascara streaked down Tracy's cheeks as Miss Dickers stood above her, arms folded, and watched her wipe away the make-up. The next time Miss Dickers' back was turned, Tracy gave her the rude finger and then looked along the row of kneeling girls. Most of the girls looked away, but Marie-Claire locked eyes with Tracy and grinned.

The next day at lunchtime PJ threw all her books into her locker and headed out into the schoolyard. She couldn't see Marie-Claire anywhere.

On the edge of the netball court, a small crowd had gathered around Meggsy Sullivan. Melinda and Jenny were standing among the onlookers and they waved at PJ to join them. Reluctantly, PJ crossed the quadrangle.

PJ didn't like Meggsy Sullivan. He had thick blond hair and a surfer's tan, and a big crowd of the Form 1 girls thought he was gorgeous, but PJ hated the way he looked straight through her as if she wasn't there.

'What is it?' asked PJ, slipping between Melinda and Jenny.

'It's Tracy Grogan's pubic hair,' said Meggsy, holding a matchbox out on the palm of his hand. Inside were two small curling light brown hairs, wispy on the grey cardboard.

'How'd you get 'em?' asked a boy.

'I felt her up, didn't I? The chicks, they all want me to finger 'em, so I take 'em down the park after school, and we get under a blanket down round them big pine trees.'

PJ groaned and turned away. Melinda and Jenny hesitated a moment before following her. When PJ sat down on the edge of the netball court, they joined her. PJ had the feeling that Melinda and Jenny were finding high school hard work. They'd stopped hanging around with the Wilson Street Primary kids and announced that 'Wellington Street Primary kids need to stick together.' But PJ knew this didn't include Marie-Claire. There was no way they would have sat down if Marie-Claire had been there.

'How can he be so gross?' said PJ, angrily. 'Tracy Grogan probably only had three pubic hairs, she's so scrawny. How can he be so mean and do that to her?'

'Have you checked out what she's done to herself lately?' asked Jenny. 'She's turned into a sharpie's chick – had her hair cut spiky with a rats-tail and all.'

'And she took the seams in on her uniform,' added Melinda. 'No way can you make a uniform cling like that if you don't especially take in the seams. I don't know why she bothered. It's not like she's got anything to show off.'

'Yeah, she looks cheap,' said Jenny.

'Cheap,' repeated Melinda, nodding.

PJ said nothing. She stood up, stretched her arms above her head, and surveyed the schoolyard.

'I think I'll go for a wander,' she said. PJ didn't mind being by herself. It was better than having to listen to Melinda and Jenny stick it to Tracy Grogan. She knew the next person they'd start bitching about would be Marie-Claire.

Lunchtime was nearly over by the time she found Marie-Claire. She was standing on the far side of the football oval beneath a stand of poplar trees, with her back to the school, her long dark hair hanging like a veil across her face. A small blonde-haired figure stood beside her and a thin wisp of cigarette smoke rose up into the air above the girls. PJ jogged across the green oval to join them. When she drew closer, she saw the flash of a match and Marie-Claire turned towards her, a lit cigarette in her hand.

'Hey, PJ, you want a ciggie?' said Tracy, offering PJ the packet. Marie-Claire turned her face away, her dark eyes half shut.

'No thanks,' said PJ, staring hard at Marie-Claire.

PJ hadn't been in the new supermarket in High Street before. Her mother shopped at Mr Armstrong's, the grocer. Mr Armstrong still sold bags of broken biscuits and delivered his customers' shopping.

Tracy, Marie-Claire and PJ stood outside the big glass windows of the supermarket, staring in at the helium balloons that were tied to every cash register.

'C'mon, let's check it out,' said Tracy. 'I need some stuff.'

'In America, they've had supermarkets for ages,' said Marie-Claire. 'And they have whole supermarkets that sell nothing but candy. They don't call them lollies there, they call them candy.'

Tracy Grogan turned and looked at Marie-Claire. 'You are such a know-it-all. What a mouth!' But then she smiled and bumped Marie-Claire on the hip in a friendly way, and Marie-Claire laughed. PJ frowned, watching the two of them with irritation as they sauntered up the aisles.

One whole section of the supermarket was full of confectionery – huge stacks of lollies in bright wrappers piled up in open glass displays. Tracy wandered past and grabbed a handful, slipping them into the pocket of her uniform. Marie-Claire looked from PJ to Tracy.

'Well, go on,' said Tracy. 'You wanted to come in here – just do it.'

Marie-Claire stared at the lollies and then plunged her hand into the bright wrappers. PJ swallowed hard. She took one small boiled sweet and slowly put it into her pocket.

Tracy rolled her eyes. 'Don't be such a mouse, PJ. You gotta grab a big handful.'

'I don't want any,' said PJ under her breath, and put the sweet back on the display. But no one heard or saw. Marie-Claire was already following Tracy down the stationery aisle, watching her with a sort of fascination.

'I need one of these for school,' said Tracy, reaching out and grabbing a mathematics set complete with pro-tractor and compass and putting it into her schoolbag. PJ felt a lunging feeling in the pit of her stomach. She looked up and down the aisle, but no one was watching.

When they came out of the supermarket, a woman was following them. Tracy looked back over her shoulder.

'We've been sprung. Run!'

The three girls raced down the footpath, diving in between shoppers. Tracy and Marie-Claire shouted to each other, laughing as they ran. PJ couldn't see anything funny about the trouble they were in. Her head was pounding. She felt as though she was going to throw up, but she kept on running. She didn't know why. *She* hadn't taken anything. But she ran anyway.

On the corner of the main shopping intersection, the three girls separated, running off in different directions. PJ knew it would be okay to slow down now, but she couldn't stop. She wanted to keep on running until she was far away from everything, until Tracy Grogan was a million miles behind her.

15

Homecoming

PJ stopped to catch her breath at the corner of Kenneth Street. Her chest ached. Her uniform felt twisted and uncomfortable and her pigtails were unravelling.

Friday was sitting on the front steps of Dr Crusoe's house, cleaning her paws, but she stopped and watched PJ as she walked past the gate. Dr Crusoe was out in the garden, watering a huge mass of briar roses.

'Ah, Miss McArdle. Just the person I was hoping to see,' she called out. 'I'm going away again next week and I was wondering . . .' She stopped. 'Are you alright, my dear?' She turned off the garden hose and crossed over to the gate, looking into PJ's face with concern.

'Fine,' said PJ, swallowing hard and trying to avoid Dr Crusoe's gaze. 'I ran all the way from the bus stop. If you'd like me to take care of Friday again, that's fine too.'

'I'll be away for about six weeks – back up to Central

Australia. It's a beautiful time of year there, after the rains with all the wildflowers in bloom. In some places the desert looks like a magic carpet of coloured petals.'

'I wish I could see it,' said PJ. 'I wish . . .'

The roar of a car engine interrupted their conversation. An old blue Holden pulled into the driveway outside PJ's house.

'Sue!' said PJ.

Sue got out of the car and walked up to the front door. She rang the doorbell, but no one answered. Sue kicked the door and rang the bell again.

''Scuse me, Dr Crusoe,' called PJ over her shoulder as she hurried across.

'What were you doing, talking to that old crow?' asked Sue crossly.

'She's not an old crow. She's really nice.'

'I hate her.'

'You don't even know her.'

'*You* don't know her, PJ. You don't know it yet but you'll find out. Old people, they hate our generation. They're shit-scared of us.'

Sue's mouth was a hard thin line, her eyes narrowed. PJ wanted to say she didn't think Dr Crusoe was scared of anyone, but it didn't seem the right moment to talk about it.

'Are you coming home? Is that why you're here? To fix things up with Mum and Dad?' she asked hopefully.

Sue laughed. 'No way, Jose!' and then, seeing PJ's face

fall, she rested one hand on her shoulder. 'Hey, I've met this great guy, Taz – he's a guitarist with this band, Wah-wah Spacemen. He's gonna be the next Jimi Hendrix. He's fantastic. I met him at Sunbury and it was love and that was it – we've been together ever since. Help me get my stuff and then you can meet him. But we've gotta be quick. I don't want to see the folks. This is perfect. I was hoping you'd be the only one home.'

Sue kept talking as she scraped her clothes out of the drawers and into cardboard boxes. She told PJ all about the concerts she'd been to over the summer, how she'd found a fabulous place to live where everyone was really laid back and no one hassled her. She was free to do whatever she wanted and she'd been offered a great job in a really swanky brothel in Elsternwick. She swept a bunch of things off her bedside table and then dumped the contents of her bedside drawer on top of them.

'What's a brothel?' asked PJ.

Sue stared at her and blinked. 'Oh, it's a kind of restaurant where they only serve soup – you know, like broth. But I don't have to serve anyone,' she said quickly. 'I only sit on the front desk and do work like a receptionist, you know, answering the phone and taking people's coats.'

A car horn tooted outside.

'That's Taz. I better go. Give us a hand, will ya?' she asked, heaving one of the boxes into her arms.

PJ and Sue stepped out of the front door at exactly the same moment that Mum walked up the driveway pushing her shopping cart. Mum stopped stock still and all the colour drained out of her face. PJ saw Sue's body stiffen but she kept moving, ignoring Mum and walking straight past her to the car.

Suddenly the box PJ was carrying grew heavy. She put her head down, staring at the ground as she followed Sue across the lawn. She felt like a traitor. Sue took the box from PJ's arms and flung it in through the open back window of the car.

'Thanks, Bubs,' she said.

'Susan,' said Mum, her voice strangely clipped and unfamiliar.

'What?' asked Sue, turning to face Mum, her fists clenched. PJ backed away from them. The air around the two women was spiky with anger.

Sue snorted. 'Don't say it,' she said, cutting Mum off before she could speak. 'I don't need your bullshit disapproval of me. You are so full of it. I don't need anything from you, so just shut your face.'

PJ put her hands over her ears and turned away. She could hear both Mum and Sue's voices rising in angry circles of outrage as she pushed open the gate and fled into Dr Crusoe's garden.

It was so quiet in Dr Crusoe's living room that the only sound PJ could hear was the pounding of her own heart. She sat on the couch, waiting for Dr Crusoe to come back from the kitchen. PJ could hardly believe that an hour ago she'd been watching Tracy and Marie-Claire shoplift from the supermarket, that only minutes earlier she'd been listening to Sue and Mum scream at each other. Being inside Dr Crusoe's house was like entering another world. Friday leapt onto the cushion beside her and stretched her long body, nuzzling her head against PJ's thigh. It was the first time the black cat had ever come that close to her, and it felt like the only good thing that had happened all day. She tentatively stroked the big cat's back. Underneath the glossy black fur, Friday's body was hard and muscular, more like a wild cat's than a domestic pet's.

PJ looked up at the *kadaicha* boots and for a moment she had a vision of herself wearing them. What had Dr Crusoe said about them? That they could make the magic man invisible? In her mind's eye, she could see herself floating above the streets of the city, skimming through Melbourne with Friday alongside her, tracking down Brian in his hiding place, following Sue back to her new house, finding Marie-Claire's house at last and casting spells over everyone – spells that would make Sue and Brian come home to stay and a spell that would make Marie-Claire lose interest in Tracy Grogan.

'You have a very faraway look about you,' said Dr Crusoe, handing PJ a cup of hot chocolate and then settling herself into the armchair opposite.

'Sorry, I mean, thanks,' said PJ, sipping the hot choco-late. 'I was sort of wishing I could make things happen.

There's all these things I'd like to do but being just a kid, well, I can't.'

'I think you're a very capable young lady. *Those who restrain desire, do so because theirs is weak enough to be restrained,*' said Dr Crusoe.

'How do you mean?' asked PJ, puzzled, wondering if she should be offended. Did Dr Crusoe think she was weak?

'I'm sorry, my dear. I'm being very obscure. That's a quote from one of my favourite poets, William Blake. Both he and I believe in action and energy. Life is about doing. If you want something, it's up to you to make it happen.'

Beneath PJ's hand, Friday began to purr, a slow rumble that vibrated up through her body.

'Oh, I get it. Like me with Friday,' said PJ, gazing down at the cat.

This time it was Dr Crusoe's turn to look puzzled.

'Well, when you first asked me to look after her, I thought she was really scary and part of me didn't want to do it. But a bigger part of me did want it. And now we even like each other. But there's all these other things. Things I want other people to do but I can't make them, and bad things I don't want them to do but I can't stop them. It's really crap.'

Dr Crusoe rested her chin on her hands and furrowed her brow in thought.

'This is quite a dilemma and I'm not sure what to advise. My friend Mr Blake would probably say *The busy bee has no time for sorrow*. That tends to be my solution to most problems, to throw myself into living. Mr Blake wrote "Energy is Eternal Delight" and I absolutely believe that.'

PJ went on quietly stroking Friday. She felt so tired, she couldn't imagine feeling energetic about anything, and she wasn't sure she understood half of what Dr Crusoe was talking about. Everything seemed too hard.

Dr Crusoe watched her, a worried expression on her face. 'I don't know if my advice has been much help in cheering you up, my dear. I have another sort of delight that I think may be more therapeutic.' As she spoke, she pulled out a small drawer in the coffee table and withdrew a dark red box.

'From Eternal Delight to Turkish Delight,' she said, offering PJ her pick of the pink, sugar-dusted sweets.

'Wow,' said PJ, brightening up. 'Thanks, Dr Crusoe.'

'Frankly, I don't think I know very much about children at all, my dear. But I can use my imagination, and perhaps that's more useful than knowing everything.'

'That's the sort of thing my friend Marie-Claire would say, that imagination is more important than knowing everything.'

'She sounds like a wise child.'

PJ thought about Marie-Claire filling her pockets with sweets at the supermarket and her face clouded with doubt. 'I hope so,' she said. 'I really hope so.'

16

Paper rounds and platform shoes

At school the next day, Marie-Claire insisted they eat lunch under the poplars on the far side of the school. A group of older students hung around there, standing in a huddle, smoking. The football oval was turning golden brown in the late summer heat, but the grass beneath the trees was soft and green. PJ stretched out on her stomach in the shade.

'Did you see Tracy this morning?' asked Marie-Claire.

'No,' said PJ, rolling onto her back and staring up through the leaves at the blue sky. 'And I don't want to see her now either.'

'Why don't you like her?' asked Marie-Claire.

'Why *do* you like her?' responded PJ. 'She thinks she's Miss Maturity. What's the big deal about pretending to be so grown-up?'

Marie-Claire pulled out a long blade of grass and rolled it between her fingers. 'I don't want to be a kid forever. It's boring. I want to do stuff. I'd go crazy if things didn't change.'

'But why do *people* have to change? My sister, Sue, she's changed so much I feel like I don't even know her anymore. It's scary. God, I hope Brian hasn't changed too.'

'Everyone changes,' said Marie-Claire. 'Especially brothers.'

'Not me,' said PJ stubbornly. 'You can count on me staying exactly the same.'

Suddenly, PJ realised that Marie-Claire had grown very quiet. She was tearing up blades of grass and shredding them into tiny pieces. It always happened when PJ mentioned anything to do with Brian. Marie-Claire would disappear inside herself. PJ felt a rush of shame at forgetting how things were for Marie-Claire. She couldn't imagine what it would be like to know that someone you loved was lost to you forever.

'Sometimes you are such a baby, PJ,' said Marie-Claire, without looking up.

'I'm sorry for talking about Brian. I know it makes you think about your brother.'

Marie-Claire's face flushed deep red. 'It's not that,' she stammered. 'It's everything. It's the way you say no all the time. I have to talk you into everything. I had to talk you into making the bathing box our place. I have to think up all the games, and now when I want us to have a new friend, I have to talk you into that too! Did Jenny and Melinda always think up everything for you too? It's always "Marie-Claire, what are we going to do now? Marie-Claire, where are we going to go now?"' she said, mimicking PJ in a shrill voice. 'When are you going to start something without me doing it for you?'

Before PJ could reply, Marie-Claire was on her feet and running across the oval. PJ wanted to shout after her, 'It's not true,' or 'You're full of crap.' But Marie-Claire was already out of earshot.

PJ walked home from school alone. It was a long walk, but it gave her time to think. By the time she pushed the back door open and stepped into the old laundry, she was feeling less angry. Mum was standing at the washing machine, forcing clothes through the mangle. Dad was always trying to talk Mum into letting him buy an automatic washer that spun the clothes but Mum said she liked to stick with what she knew. PJ watched as Mum hoisted the laundry basket onto her hip.

'Is everything alright, Pauline?' she said, stopping to gaze into PJ's grumpy face.

'Fine,' lied PJ. 'Do you want me to do that for you, Mum?'

Mum looked startled. She put one hand up to her forehead. 'I do have a headache,' she said. 'But I'd better do it myself. You're not old enough yet.'

'Mum! I can do this. It's only pegging out washing, not brain surgery.'

'No double-pegging then, Bubs,' she said, reluctantly handing over the basket.

'Sheesh,' said PJ to herself as she plonked the laundry basket down next to the clothes line. What was wrong with her family? Didn't they think she could do anything? She lifted her dad's shirt out of the basket and pegged it up in the breeze, jamming the pegs down hard. The next time someone called her 'Bubs' she was going to scream.

PJ walked into the newsagency and waited at the counter.

'I've come about the ad,' she said. 'About doing the paper round.'

The proprietor was a big man with a red face and a loud check shirt. He wiped one hand across his thinning hair.

'Sorry, we don't take girls.'

'Why not? I can ride a bike as good as any boy. I've got my big brother's Herald Boy Racer. Girls can fold up newspapers too. I've got everything I need, and I know every street around here.' She put her hands in the pockets of her jeans and tried to look tough.

'Keen, aren't you?' he said.

'Very,' she replied.

'Get your parents to give me a call,' he said, writing a number on a piece of paper and giving it to PJ. Then he turned to serve a customer.

It took a week to talk Mum and Dad around. It was as if they couldn't hear PJ as she sat at the kitchen table trying to make them see why she needed the round.

'You let Brian do a paper round when he was only eleven, and I'm nearly thirteen.'

'That was different,' said Mum, visibly flinching at the mention of Brian's name. 'He's a boy.'

'It's not very ladylike, love,' added her Dad.

'I don't want to be ladylike. Besides, this is 1973, girls aren't like that now. Leastways, I'm not.'

PJ had wanted to boast about getting the round to Marie-Claire but by the time she had talked Mum and Dad around, the fight with Marie-Claire had blown over and she didn't want to stir it up again. They'd tried to stay mad at each other. PJ had spent two lunchtimes sitting with Melinda and Jenny while Marie-Claire and Tracy sat on the far side of the oval, smoking cigarettes. But on the third day, PJ had arrived at school and found Marie-Claire waiting beside her locker, and suddenly, the fight was over.

Every night after school, PJ took her bike out of the shed and pedalled straight down to the newsagent's as fast as she could. She loaded the evening papers into Brian's saddlebags and pedalled out into the afternoon sunlight. The bike was heavy beneath her but it made her feel strong and confident that she could do it. No one could call her a baby now. It took an hour and a half and an extra trip back to the newsagent's to get the round done, and every day she'd try to knock a few minutes off the time. Her hands were always black with newspaper ink and her legs ached from pedalling by the time she was finished, but it was a good, warm sort of ache and she liked to think of the black ink as a badge of honour.

PJ was waiting for the lights to change when she saw Sue down the street waving at a taxi. As she stepped out into the road, her ankle twisted, and for a panic-stricken moment PJ thought Sue was going to fall right in front of the approaching taxi. Luckily she fell backwards into the gutter. The taxi sped by, ignoring her. PJ pedalled up as fast as she could to Sue, who sat in the gutter, head in hands, sobbing.

'You okay?' asked PJ.

Sue looked up. Long black streaks of mascara ran down her cheeks.

'Bubs? What are you doing here?'

'I just finished my paper round and I was going home.'

'Look, they're broken,' said Sue, picking up one five-inch platform shoe and examining the straps. 'And I think I've twisted my ankle. That bastard taxi driver – he didn't even stop. What am I gonna do?'

'Do you want me to call Taz for you? Maybe he could come down and pick you up.'

'Don't mention that name to me ever again,' she said, her voice flat and tired.

'Well,' said PJ, drawing breath. 'Maybe I could dink you back to your place.'

Sue was cradling the broken shoe in her hands. She didn't speak for a moment. Finally she looked up.

'Would you do that for me?' she said in a small voice.

''Course,' said PJ, embarrassed. She hated seeing Sue like this – pathetic and tired instead of her usual fiery self. Shakily, Sue got to her feet, one platform shoe still strapped to her left foot. She positioned herself side-saddle on the crossbar of the bike, and then PJ reached around her awkwardly to grab the handlebars. PJ could feel Sue's weight dragging the bike down as she pushed off, but weeks of newspaper deliveries had made her legs strong and she pedalled on furiously.

'Left down this street,' said Sue. 'It's number 16.'

They stopped outside an old double-fronted weather-board house. The fence was broken in a couple of places and the front verandah was covered with piles of junk – broken chairs, rolled-up carpet and scrap metal.

'Do you wanna come in for a cuppa?' asked Sue.

PJ followed her down the side path and in the back door. The house stank of cigarette smoke, old cooking smells and some other musty odour that PJ couldn't place. All the blinds were pulled down, and in the half-light it was hard to make out what was happening on the posters and dark swirling pictures that covered the living-room walls. Sue flopped down on the couch and a cloud of dust rose up around her. She pushed aside the over-flowing ashtrays so she could lift her sore ankle onto the coffee table.

'Why don't you grab a glass and fix yourself some-thing, Bubs – I mean PJ?'

PJ nodded and went into the kitchen, a tiny galley with a couple of small counters either side of an old Kooka stove. The sink was overflowing with dishes and the tap dripped incessantly. A thick trail of ants was pouring in through the window and swarming over the counter. PJ pulled the fridge door open. Inside there were only a couple of cans of VB, a small bowl with something furry growing in it, and a limp bunch of celery in the bottom of the crisper.

PJ pulled open the cupboards, looking for a glass or cup, but most of the crockery was piled up in the sink. There was hardly any food anywhere. An empty packet of Cornflakes, a tin of beans and a bottle of tomato sauce sat on one of the counters among a litter of wrap-pings. PJ washed out two cups and filled them with fresh water.

'It's kind of . . . interesting, this place,' said PJ, trying to think of something complimentary to say to Sue as she handed her the cup of water.

'The guys in this house, they're animals. Fuzz is the worst, his room is like a dog's kennel. No one ever cleans up anything except me, and I don't want to get stuck doing that for the whole lot of them, so I avoid it too.'

When she'd finished the water, PJ helped Sue to her room. It was tiny. There was a double mattress covered in bright red sheets on the floor and an old tea chest with an incense burner on it. The walls were bare except for a poster of David Bowie pinned above the bed.

Sue lay down on the mattress and stared at the ceiling with a desolate expression. PJ lay down beside her.

'Why don't you come home?' asked PJ.

'They don't want me back, kiddo. They don't even want you to see me.'

'That's not true,' said PJ. She wanted to sound firm but it came out sounding uncertain.

Sue laughed bitterly. 'PJ, you've got to promise me one thing. Promise you won't tell them where I am. No matter what. Like Mum always said, I've made my bed and now I've gotta lie in it.' She shut her eyes and for a minute PJ thought she'd drifted off to sleep, until she saw a tear make a shimmering trail down Sue's cheek.

17

Good deeds

PJ and Marie-Claire sat on the back steps of Dr Crusoe's house with Friday between them, both stroking the cat's thick black fur.

'What are you feeding this cat? She's getting really fat,' said Marie-Claire.

'Sometimes I give her chocolate,' said PJ guiltily.

'I thought you didn't like her.'

'She didn't like me, but now she does.'

'Things change,' said Marie-Claire teasingly.

PJ grunted.

'Speaking of change, when are we going to go back to your house for a change? We always come here. Do you realise I've still never been there?'

This time it was Marie-Claire who grunted. 'It's not a good time.'

'Has Tracy been back to your house?' asked PJ crossly.

'I told you, no one's allowed to come back to my place at the moment. My dad's got that recurring disease that he caught when he was working in Africa. Anyway, it's flared up again. I'm not allowed to have friends back. He has to have absolute quiet. When he's not sick, then you can come back.'

'Well, couldn't we stay outside and then I could meet your pony.'

'Silver is out on agistment.'

'But we *always* come to my house. It would be good to go somewhere different.'

'How about Sue's place? It sounds grouse. Why don't we go there after school some time and visit her?'

PJ shifted uncomfortably on the step. She was starting to wish she hadn't told Marie-Claire about Sue. But she'd had to tell someone. 'That's not what I meant.'

'What's wrong with going to your sister's? I wish we lived in a share house.'

PJ sighed. 'It's okay. But it's kind of grotty. And I told her I wouldn't tell anyone about it, so I'd have to have a good excuse to take you there.'

They both sat with their elbows on their knees and chins in their hands, thinking.

'I've got an idea,' said Marie-Claire slowly. 'You said before that Sue's really skinny-looking and there was nothing in the fridge at her place. You've got heaps of money saved, haven't you?'

'Yeah, so?' said PJ.

'Well, you could buy Sue something really nice to eat and go round and I could cook her a meal and we could both clean up the kitchen for her. You could say I'm your helper. I could cook my special omelette. It's really yummy. What do you reckon?'

They met in High Street and filled two shopping bags with groceries from the supermarket. Marie-Claire slipped a few lollies into her pockets from the sweet counter.

'Why do you do that? You don't have to. I have heaps of money. I'll buy you some, if you want.'

'Look, Moneybags McArdle,' said Marie-Claire. 'I can take care of myself. Besides, it's not about the money.'

'It's about being an idiot,' said PJ under her breath.

Sue was still in bed when they got to her house, even though it was 4.30 in the afternoon. PJ knocked gently on her bedroom door. Marie-Claire and PJ sat on the end of Sue's mattress and tipped the bag of groceries out. PJ had worried that Sue would be angry with her, especially about telling Marie-Claire, but Sue liked Marie-Claire straight away.

'She's a bit of a little spunk, your friend,' Sue whispered in PJ's ear as they carried the bags of groceries into the kitchen.

'Don't you do anything, Sue,' said Marie-Claire.

'Thanks, honey-bunnies,' she laughed. 'I'll jump under the shower.'

Fuzz was stretched out on the couch, rolling thin cigarettes, one after the other, blowing smoke rings into the air above his head. He looked across and snarled at PJ and Marie-Claire as they bustled about in the little galley kitchen. 'You two Girl Guides or something? Doing your good deeds for the day?'

'Ignore him,' called Sue, putting her head around the bathroom door. 'He's just jealous.'

Marie-Claire washed and PJ dried and organised space in the cupboards for the big pile of dishes. Fuzz kept coming in and out of the kitchen and shaking his head as if he disapproved. When PJ pulled up the blind and started cleaning the kitchen window, he groaned and shaded his eyes.

'You guys are nuts,' he said. He reached over Marie-Claire's head to get a cup. Suddenly, he stopped and parted his thick mane of hair, peering at Marie-Claire with bloodshot eyes.

'Hey, aren't you Kooky Kev's little sis?' asked Fuzz.

'No!' said Marie-Claire, turning away from him with disgust. She flung the dishrag into the sink and squatted down to search the lower cupboards for a frypan. By the time Sue emerged from the shower, Marie-Claire had finished cooking the omelette and turned it out onto a plate. Sue sat with the plate on her lap on the beaten-up old couch. PJ and Marie-Claire pushed a pile of old magazines off the coffee table and sat side by side, watching her.

'This is great. You guys can have no idea how much I miss real food,' said Sue, as she wolfed down the omelette. 'I've been living on Twisties and V-8 juice.'

'Why don't you come home, then?' asked PJ.

Sue looked at PJ with annoyance. 'You don't get it, kiddo, do you?'

'No, I don't,' said PJ. 'Mum and Dad miss you. Me too.'

'Don't you ever give up?' asked Sue, exasperated. She put the plate of food down on the arm of the couch and walked into her bedroom, slamming the door behind her.

Fuzz flopped down on the couch.

'She's a wildcat, that sister of yours,' he said, laughing. 'Hey, you chicks want to support a good cause, why don't you cook me some of that grub?'

PJ scowled. 'Let's get out of here,' she said to Marie-Claire.

Outside in the cool early evening, PJ dragged her bike into the street.

'Hop on,' she said. Marie-Claire balanced herself on the crossbar of the bike and they cycled off along the street.

'How come Sue sleeps all day?' asked Marie-Claire. 'Does she work at night or something?'

'Not anymore. She was a receptionist in a brothel, but she said they wanted her to serve the food and so she quit. Dumb reason for quitting, if you ask me.'

'A brothel!' said Marie-Claire, her eyes wide.

'Yeah, you know, one of those soup restaurants.'

'They don't make soup in a brothel.'

'If you're so smart, what do they make?'

Marie-Claire blushed and spoke in a whisper. 'PJ, a brothel is a place where men go and pay to have sex.'

PJ slammed on the brakes and Marie-Claire only just managed to catch her balance as she slipped off the crossbar. PJ's cheeks were flaming.

'Why do you have to be such a know-it-all?' she shouted at Marie-Claire.

'I'm not a know-it-all. I only knew that one thing.'

'So I guess you know more about my sister than me. I feel so stupid! Why did she lie?'

'She probably didn't want to upset you. Look, I don't want to fight with you, PJ,' cried Marie-Claire, exasperated. 'Especially not about your sister. That's dumb.'

PJ folded her arms and turned her back on Marie-Claire, glaring at the lengthening shadows. She bit her lip, trying to fight back tears.

'I want things to be the way they used to be,' said PJ. 'I want things to be good for Sue. I really want to help her but I don't know how.'

'You'll think of something. You gotta stop worrying. Let's do something fun, the two of us. Let's have an adventure, just you and me.'

'We could go and play in the bathing box, like last summer,' said PJ hopefully.

'Nah. I don't want to play cubbies anymore. That's kids' stuff. Let's go to the movies or something. In the city. We could go and see *Alvin Purple*.'

'They wouldn't let us in. We're not old enough.'

'We could sneak in. *Alvin Purple* looks really funny and groovy too,' said Marie-Claire.

'Groovy? Duh. Can't we see something else?'

Marie-Claire scowled and was about to say something but then changed her mind.

'Okay,' said Marie-Claire. 'I want to do what you want to do. Great minds think alike so we'll do something great, something really exciting that will make you forget all your hassles. You and me are never going to have another argument about anything ever again.'

'Never ever again,' agreed PJ.

18

The power of no

PJ ran all the way from Kenneth Street to the station. There was no way she was going to miss the train. It was the first time her mum had agreed to let her go into the city for the day without an adult. Ever since the fight with Sue on the front lawn, Mum had started saying 'Yes, dear,' to everything, as if 'no' was a word too hard to pronounce.

The train pulled into the station and Marie-Claire hung out the window waving. PJ felt her heart sink as Tracy Grogan leaned forward and pushed the door open for her. She climbed into the carriage, sat down beside Marie-Claire and whispered, 'Why do we have to go with Tracy? I thought you said it would be just us two. Three's a crowd.'

'No it's not – we're like the Three Musketeers. She can be Porthos and I'll be Athos and you can be Aramis,' replied Marie-Claire in a low voice.

PJ didn't know anything about the Three Musketeers, but she tried to shrug off her disappointment. She wasn't going to let having Tracy along wreck the day.

Tracy put her feet up on the green vinyl seat, took out a black texta and drew a smiley face on the seat beside her. The vinyl had already been slashed and sewn up again with big black stitches, so she drew jagged lines like lightning strikes stretching from each carefully repaired stitch. Marie-Claire laughed and tried to catch PJ's eye. PJ looked out the window as the train rattled its way towards the city and wished a train inspector would come into the carriage and spring Tracy.

When the train went over the Yarra, they all hung out the open window and looked down into the yellow water. Further along, in another carriage, two boys were climbing out the window, hooting at the girls. Tracy waved at them.

'Hey, what d'ya reckon? Let's force the door between the carriages and go and talk to them.'

'We don't want to get stuck with them hanging around with us all day. They look like a pack of dickheads,' said PJ, retreating into the carriage and folding her arms across her chest. Marie-Claire looked from Tracy to PJ and frowned.

'Yeah, let's not,' she said, offering a small smile to PJ.

At Flinders Street station they walked up the ramp to the street and Tracy spat a thick wad of spittle onto the wall.

'Didn't you see the sign, "No spitting"?' said PJ, annoyed.

''Course I did,' said Tracy. 'That's why I spat.'

PJ felt like she was walking along Swanston Street inside a big black cloud. When they stopped outside the Darrell Lea chocolate shop, she tried to make herself feel excited about the display of sweets. She bought a big bag of Rocklea Road and the three girls gorged themselves as they window-shopped.

'Let's go to Myer's,' said Tracy.

'I thought we were going to the movies,' said PJ. 'That's what I told my mum I was doing. She'll be pissed off with me if all I do is wander around the city.'

'So what?' said Tracy. 'I told my mum I was going to Marie-Claire's place to do homework! Myer's is more fun than the flicks.'

PJ turned to Marie-Claire and grimaced, as if to say 'I told you so,' but Marie-Claire just shrugged.

Tracy led the way. She looked sassy and confident, swanning around the cosmetics department and fiddling with things on each display. She tried the lipstick testers first, putting slashes of colour on the inside of her wrist. When she'd found the brightest red, she stuck her bum out and pouted into the mirrors on the counter as she applied the colour.

'C'mon guys, try something. That's what they're there for!' she said.

Marie-Claire chose a bright orange one. PJ thought it made her look sickly but Marie-Claire pouted at her reflection in the mirrors and then laughed with pleasure.

PJ reached for a pale pink, smudging a little bit on her teeth by accident as she applied it.

'Here, PJ,' said Tracy, approaching her with a powder puff. 'Let's get rid of them freckles of yours,' said Tracy. PJ shut her eyes and wished she could stop hating Tracy.

When they'd finished with all the Revlon products and the attendant was starting to get edgy, they moved on to the next counter.

'This is the gear I really want,' said Tracy, stopping in front of the Mary Quant display. Tracy tried everything: lipsticks, eyeliners, mascara, and long sticks of black kohl until she looked as though she'd been punched in both eyes, more ghoulish than gorgeous. The cosmetics attendant approached them and snapped angrily.

'You girls, what do you think you're doing?'

'They say "testers",' said Marie-Claire, sweetly. 'And that's what we're doing, testing them.'

'We don't want your crap products anyway,' said Tracy, spinning around and heading towards the escalators.

PJ started to feel sick. Her mouth was tacky with the taste of lipstick, and the chocolate and marshmallow Rocklea Road churned around in her stomach. Marie-Claire and Tracy ignored her as she stood behind them on the escalator. PJ could feel her cheeks burning under the thick veneer of foundation and powder that Tracy had slathered on her.

In the Miss Shop, they trawled through the racks. PJ

didn't feel like trying anything on, but Marie-Claire and Tracy wandered around with armloads of things until they found an out-of-the-way change room where there was no attendant. They squashed into the same booth together while PJ stood outside and listened to them giggling and whispering. She slumped against the wall and caught a glimpse of herself in a long mirror. She looked like a weird clown, the red rouge clashing with her hair, her eyes surrounded with an arc of bright green eye shadow. She turned away and noticed a man in a suit wandering among the blouses. He stopped and looked at PJ with curiosity. She quickly turned and banged on the change-room door.

When Tracy came out of the booth, she adjusted her clothes. They looked twisted and bulky.

'You've got that red top on underneath. The one that you were looking at before. You're pinching it, aren't you?' said PJ angrily.

'Shhh,' Tracy hissed, glaring at PJ.

Marie-Claire emerged from the change room with all her clothes and hung them on the return rack.

'Too ordinary,' she said. 'We're not that sort of ordinary. Let's pretend we're really rich and go up and look at the evening gowns.'

PJ followed them up to the third floor. The man who had been watching her in the Miss Shop was on the escalator below them and PJ glanced at him and felt a shiver of unease.

In the evening-wear department, Marie-Claire ran her hands across the fabrics, stroking the silks and satins, her eyes glowing with excitement.

'I want this,' she said, pulling out a sky-blue chiffon dress. It was tie-dyed with swirling white patterns that looked like clouds against the blue silk. Reluctantly, PJ followed the other girls into the change rooms. Marie-Claire stepped out of the cubicle with the dress on and spread the folds of fabric out on either side of her, like the wings of a giant blue butterfly. The silk wafted and swirled as she spun one way and then the other in front of the mirror.

'You look grouse,' said Tracy. PJ nodded in agreement. Marie-Claire did look incredible, like a fairy princess from a picture book with her long dark hair falling loosely around bare shoulders, the folds of blue and white silk hanging gracefully across her body.

'If you want it, take it,' said Tracy.

Marie-Claire looked at them both, her eyes bright. PJ felt a leaden thunk in the pit of her stomach.

'Go on. You look sexy and all,' said Tracy. 'You should have it.' She looked at PJ, defying her to say anything.

'Don't, Marie-Claire,' pleaded PJ. 'Just don't. It's stealing.'

Tracy laughed. 'Don't be a wanker, PJ. It's not like Myer's are gonna miss it. They make millions and billions of dollars every day. What's one dress?' said Tracy.

Marie-Claire didn't comment. She slipped back into

the cubicle and came out a minute later with the evening gown rolled up into a ball. Tracy took it from her and stuffed it into the small pink plastic bag she had slung over her shoulder.

'But what if we're caught?' said PJ, desperate not to leave the change rooms.

'No big deal,' said Tracy. 'We'll say we were buying it. They can't arrest you until you leave the store.'

They took another escalator up to the next floor, and PJ watched in despair as Tracy and Marie-Claire began fingering everything they passed and glancing at each other with conspiratorial glee. Now that they were in the mood, they began picking up whatever took their fancy. A cheap silver necklace, a pink plastic belt, a bottle of dark red nail polish, all disappeared into Tracy's pink bag. PJ followed behind them, feeling nauseous. When they took the escalator to the floor that sold haberdashery, she noticed that the big man with the beer belly spilling over his belt was still behind them.

'That man, I reckon he's watching us. He knows you've been pinching stuff and he's going to dob us all in.'

'Don't be paranoid. He's probably shopping,' said Marie-Claire.

'What was he doing in the ladies' underwear department then? And the Miss Shop too?'

'Maybe he's a pervert,' said Marie-Claire dismissively.

'No, she's right,' said Tracy, watching him. 'He's following us. He's a dick.'

'A what?' asked PJ, frowning.

'A store detective,' said Tracy, shifting the pink bag from one shoulder to the other. There was a long moment of silence.

'What are we gonna do?' whispered PJ.

Marie-Claire wouldn't look at PJ. She turned to Tracy, waiting for her decision. PJ wanted to slap her, to take her by the arm and drag her away from Tracy, onto the escalators and out into the street where they'd be away from it all.

'I've got an idea,' said Tracy. 'Follow me.'

As they moved through the haberdashery section, Tracy lifted a big pair of shearing scissors off the rack and slipped them into the pink bag.

'Quick, back to the ladies' rest room. He can't follow us in there.'

It was incredibly squashy in the toilet cubicle. PJ stood on the seat to make more room, one foot on either side of the bowl. Tracy and Marie-Claire pulled the long dress out of the bag. The blue silk fell in folds at their feet. All three of them stared at the evening gown.

'We could put it back on the rack,' suggested PJ.

'Nah, he'll spring us as soon as we step out of here,' said Tracy.

'I thought you said he can't do that until we leave the store,' said Marie-Claire.

'Maybe he can't. I don't know for sure. We've got a lot of stuff now. We're gonna have to get rid of it. Fast!'

131

They all began talking at once.

'Shut up!' Tracy almost shouted. She pulled out the sewing shears and held them up. 'See these? They're gonna fix everything.' She grabbed a fold of the blue evening dress and cut off a long strip of silk.

'What are you *doing*?' asked PJ, appalled.

'What does it look like, moron?' snapped Tracy, throwing the strip of fabric into the toilet bowl. 'We're getting rid of the evidence.'

'This is really dumb, Marie-Claire,' said PJ. Marie-Claire said nothing. She stared at the strips of fabric that were piling up in the toilet bowl, her dark eyes wide, as if she were hypnotised.

'It's too late now. Shut up!' said Tracy. 'Just shut up and flush the bloody toilet.' Suddenly, she didn't look so calm and confident. She was trembling.

PJ pushed the handle. *I am an accomplice*, she thought, as the strips of blue and white silk were sucked down around the U-bend. PJ stood staring at the toilet bowl as Tracy cut more strips off and dropped them into the water. She glanced across, but Marie-Claire wouldn't meet PJ's eyes. She was staring into the toilet.

'You guys are sick,' said PJ. 'I'm going home.'

'Yeah, why don't you?' said Tracy.

As PJ fumbled with the latch, Marie-Claire reached out and grabbed her arm. 'No, don't go,' she said. 'Everything's going to be okay.'

'It's not okay,' shouted PJ. 'You've wrecked everything!'

'Oh for God's sake,' said Tracy, wrenching open the toilet door. 'Piss off, Miss Goody-Two-Shoes. Good riddance. Who needs ya?' Tracy pushed PJ out of the cubicle and slammed the door shut behind her.

PJ didn't look to see if the store detective was watching her. She didn't care if he caught her. She stared at her reflection in the shop windows as she walked down Swanston Street to the railway station. She could feel tears make a hot trail through the thick, powdery make-up.

The train rattled out of Flinders Street station and down towards the bay. PJ sat on the edge of her seat. Her whole body felt numb with rage, but slowly the rhythm of the train soothed her. She got off at Brighton Beach station and walked down to the old green bathing box. The sky and sea were both slate-grey. There wasn't a ripple on the surface of the bay. When she reached the bathing box, she found that someone had set the half-collapsed one beside it on fire, leaving blackened stumps jutting out of the water. PJ kicked at the rotten charred wood and a spray of water flew into the air along with the charcoal. All of a sudden, it seemed that was the way everything was going. Everything was burnt out and ruined.

Neither she nor Marie-Claire had been to the bathing box since school had started. She pushed the door open. Inside, all the cushions were damp. The room had a desolate abandoned air. For the rest of the afternoon,

PJ sat on the floor, tracing patterns in the wind-drifts of sand that speckled the wooden floor and watching the play of dull winter light across the weatherboards.

19

Friendship on ice

At lunchtime, PJ headed straight to the canteen. If you got in early, you could get the first hot-dogs, before the frankfurters dried out. There was a lot of shoving once the queue built up. PJ bought three hot-dogs, one each for herself, Melinda and Jenny, and carried them out into the schoolyard. Melinda and Jenny were sitting on a bench in the shade. They wriggled apart to make space for PJ to sit between them and took their hot-dogs.

'I love how crusty this bread is,' said Jenny, biting into the hot-dog.

'Thanks, PJ,' said Melinda, through a mouthful of food. 'It's great to have you back.'

'I haven't been anywhere,' said PJ.

'You know what I mean,' said Melinda.

PJ hadn't spoken to Marie-Claire in weeks. On the Monday after their Myer's escapade, PJ moved down the

135

front of the classroom, to the seat behind Melinda and Jenny. It was almost like being in primary school again, the three of them together through lunch and recess. Occasionally PJ would spot Marie-Claire and Tracy wandering across the oval to where the smokers hid under the poplar trees. The two of them sat together for every class now, right up the back of the room, though they both seemed to spend a lot of time out of class, sitting outside Miss Dickers' office.

Melinda and Jenny wanted PJ to do everything with them. They even talked her into joining their ice-skating club.

'I won't have to wear some tizzy little skirt or anything, will I?' asked PJ. 'I can go in my jeans?'

'Sure, if you want,' said Melinda.

'Boy, you're just the same,' said Jenny. 'I thought when you changed your name to PJ and started hanging around with Marie-Claire and that horrible Tracy Grogan, you were going to get more . . .' She waved her hand about in the air in a vague gesture.

'More what?' asked PJ.

'You know, less of a tomboy, more mature or something,' she said.

'No way. I am never going to change like that, ever. And anyway, those two aren't mature, or anything. They're a couple of dickheads.'

Melinda's mum came by and picked PJ up after lunch on Saturday. PJ slid into the back seat beside the other girls. Melinda was wearing a short orange skirt like a netball skirt with pleats. Her long blonde hair was neatly braided, her hands were folded into a fluffy white muff, and her very own pair of pristine white skates sat in a white carrybag at her feet. Jenny had a skirt on as well, but she didn't have her own skates.

They all piled out of the car outside the St Moritz ice-skating rink. A crowd of teenagers were lined up on the steps waiting to get in.

A blast of cold air hit them as they passed into the rink. PJ stood staring out over the ice at a shaft of sunlight that shone down through the glass domed roof, illuminating one end of the rink. PJ remembered Brian bringing her here once, when she was really little. He had spent the whole afternoon skating with her, holding both her hands and skating backwards ahead of her, catching her every time she fell. It was so long since she'd seen Brian, she could hardly remember what his face looked like.

'C'mon,' said Jenny, nudging her, 'let's go get our skates.'

Melinda and Jenny stepped straight onto the rink and slid effortlessly into the centre where the best skaters were pirouetting, while PJ clung to the rails, trying to avoid the other inexpert skaters thudding into the black rubber walls. She was just getting the hang of moving on the ice when an announcement came over the loudspeaker that it was time for the fast men skaters to take the rink. A gang of sharpies elbowed their way past the retreating crowds of girls and older skaters, and Suzi Quatro's voice blasted out across from the loudspeakers. A puddle in the lower corner grew larger as the boys shaved ice with their blades, taking the corners in a blur of speed.

PJ clumped over to where Melinda and Jenny were sitting with a group of other girls. The skating club girls all had little white cards with stars punched into them for each time they achieved a new technique, and they linked arms and skated around together, practising fancy moves. When the speed racing was over, Jenny and Melinda each grabbed PJ by an arm and led her out into the centre of the rink.

'I don't know if I'm ready for this,' said PJ. Her ankles were already aching.

An older girl was practising pirouettes right next to them. It made PJ giddy to watch.

'I think I'd like to take a break,' she said finally, her legs aching, her bum damp from countless falls on the ice.

'We'll help you back to the edge of the rink,' said Melinda, taking her arm authoritatively.

'I'm not that klutzy. I can do it myself,' said PJ, trying to shrug her arm free without losing her balance.

'You are so stubborn, PJ McArdle. You'd bite your nose off to spite your face.'

Jenny and Melinda linked arms and skated backwards away from her, shaking their heads. PJ struggled doggedly across the huge expanse of ice. By the time she reached the rails again and clambered off the ice, she was wet all over and her hands were red raw with cold.

At the kiosk, PJ bought herself a Violet Crumble and sat alone at the far end of the rink, chipping the chocolate off the honeycomb with her teeth, watching the skaters circle the rink. Suddenly, everyone began skating towards her, streaming across the ice and hitting the wall in front of her. PJ became aware that someone was shouting behind her, and other angry voices were rising above the sound of the music. She turned and saw two sharpies circling each other, while a girl stood between them, screaming for them to stop. One of the boys had been hit in the nose already, and blood was streaming over his lip. He wiped it away with the back of his hands, staring at his own blood with outrage. Suddenly he took the skates that were slung over his shoulder and swung them by the bootlaces. The blades slashed into the other boy's face, cutting it wide open, in a gash that ran from eyebrow to lip. Blood spurted out, flecking the icy puddles of silvery water. The boy fell to the ground, clutching his face, and the other sharpie laid into him with heavy black boots, kicking until the wounded boy was on his side, convulsing. PJ's stomach lurched, but as she turned, something about the screaming girl caught her eye.

It was as if everything went silent and she couldn't hear what the girl was screaming, only see her open mouth. It was Tracy Grogan. Tracy's white T-shirt was splattered with blood and her face was distorted with grief and fear. Her hands were clenched and pressed against her cheeks, as if she wanted to hurt herself, Suddenly, Marie-Claire was there, slipping one arm around Tracy. She looked up, and for a moment her eyes locked with PJ's before she turned Tracy away from the fight and forced a path through the crowd. PJ pushed her way back through the milling onlookers, onto the ice, and skated out into the whiteness.

20

The gift

'Do you know what I heard?' said Melinda, her voice dropping to a hushed whisper. 'Tracy Grogan's been expelled!'

It was Friday morning and Tracy hadn't been at school all week. A light rain was falling on the school grounds, and Melinda, Jenny and PJ sat on a bench in the covered area underneath the auditorium, eating cream buns.

'That's not what I heard,' said Jenny, licking a blob of cream from her fingers. 'I heard she got taken out of school because she's pregnant.'

Melinda looked scandalised but PJ shook her head. 'She can't be pregnant. She's never even had her periods yet.' Even though she hated Tracy, she still didn't like the way Melinda and Jenny talked about her.

PJ spotted Marie-Claire at a distance, sitting alone on the edge of the oval. PJ swallowed the last mouthful of her bun and stood up.

'Where are you going?' asked Jenny.

'I won't be long.'

Marie-Claire looked up, startled, as PJ approached.

'Hi,' said Marie-Claire, slightly puzzled.

'Hello,' replied PJ.

'You want to come up to the poplar trees?' asked Marie-Claire.

'No,' said PJ. 'I just thought I'd see what's up with you.'

Marie-Claire sighed and looked away.

'If you're looking for the gossip about Tracy,' she said, 'I don't have anything to say.'

'I'm not interested in Tracy. I didn't want to be her friend. I was your friend.'

'Friends don't run out on each other. That day in Myer's, you didn't have to run away like that. I know it was a mess, but you didn't make it easier, hanging back, making me do all the work, being nice to you and being nice to Tracy and you not helping one little bit, always disapproving and sneering.'

'You were the one who brought Tracy along. You know she likes to shoplift, and you played along with it all the way.'

'It was just a bit of fun.'

'It wasn't my idea of fun.'

Marie-Claire rolled her eyes. 'What's wrong with you? Why do you disapprove of everything I do these days? We were meant to be best friends forever.'

'It wasn't me who changed,' said PJ. She turned to walk away.

'Look,' said Marie-Claire, touching her lightly on the arm, 'do you want to come down the beach on Saturday? We could hang around in the bathing box. Be like summer. Like the olden days.'

'Is Tracy coming?'

'Not if you don't want her to.'

'Okay,' said PJ. 'That would be good.'

On Saturday morning, walking down through the ti-trees, PJ felt a rush of the pleasure of last summer. There was no one else on the beach except a man and a dog in the distance. The sky was grey and overcast and the sand cool beneath her feet. She took off her desert boots and waded through the ice-cold water.

Marie-Claire was waiting for PJ inside the bathing box, sweeping away the sand that had settled on the table. In one hand she held a cigarette, its tip glowing in the dim light of the windowless bathing box. Her long dark hair was tied back in a ponytail, and she looked thinner than usual.

'You want a fag?' asked Marie-Claire.

'I don't smoke.'

'Go on. It won't hurt to try one.'

She took a crumpled packet of cigarettes out of the

pocket of her denim jacket and extracted a half-smoked cigarette. There was a faint impression of lipstick around the edge of the filter.

'Someone's already smoked half of that,' said PJ.

'Yeah, I pinched them from an ashtray. They were only half used up. Seemed stupid to waste them.'

'Gross,' said PJ. She screwed her face up and handed back the cigarette butt.

Marie-Claire frowned and took a small puff of her cigarette.

'Look, I know you're pissed off at me and I want to sort of make it up to you, so . . .' She reached around behind her folding chair, pulled out a cardboard box, and pushed it towards PJ.

'Here, I got you this,' she said, grinning.

PJ stared at the box in disbelief. It was the size of a packing crate. Marie-Claire had stuck sea shells on the top and tied a long piece of coloured wool around the box as a ribbon. PJ undid the knot. Inside was another box. She looked up at Marie-Claire and laughed. The second box had black stars drawn on it in texta and a piece of white kitchen string tied around it. There were three more boxes to get through until she found something wrapped in tissue paper inside the fifth box. She unfolded the layers of tissue paper carefully, but even before she'd lifted the last layer she realised, with a sinking feeling, what was inside. Lying in her lap, nestled in the tissue paper, was a pair of *kadaicha* boots.

'Where did you get these?' she demanded angrily.

'Don't say thank you,' said Marie-Claire. 'I thought you'd really like them. That's why I got them for you.'

'They're not yours to give. They belong to Dr Crusoe. You stole them.'

'You don't know that, I might have bought them for you,' said Marie-Claire, folding her arms across her chest and sticking her chin out.

'But you didn't buy these,' said PJ.

'I didn't exactly steal them,' said Marie-Claire sullenly.

'Well, what exactly did you do?'

'This is crap. You always make me feel as if you're so much better than me. You've done it too – gone inside people's houses and stuff.'

'We only *visited* when we played the visiting game. We didn't steal. Anyway, I knew even that was wrong. It was always your idea.'

'Me again. I'm the bad guy. You were always happy to play along. You loved it. Now you make me feel like I'm always wrong about everything. You wanted those boots. You told me how you wanted them.'

'And now Dr Crusoe will think that I stole them. I should never have shown you where the key was. You've wrecked everything again.'

PJ looked down at the pair of *kadaicha* boots and bit her lip so hard that she could taste her own blood, and then thrust the box back at Marie-Claire.

'Here, take them back. I don't want them.'

'You're going to dob me in, aren't you?' said Marie-Claire bitterly. She wrapped her arms around the box on her lap. A wedge of sunlight cut across her face making her dark eyes fierce and bright. 'I want things to be like they were before,' shouted Marie-Claire. 'I want us to be friends like we used to be.'

'I wanted that too,' shouted PJ.

'Then why do you keep putting me down? Why have you gone back to that prissy Melinda and Jenny? Why don't you want to do anything with me anymore?'

'It's not you – it's the stuff you do.'

'You used to like it – you liked everything, you wanted to come with me and do things and have fun together.'

'What? Steal and lie and smoke grotty half-smoked cigarettes? That's not fun, that's just stupid.' She snatched Marie-Claire's cigarette butt, threw it on the floor of the bathing box and stamped on it. 'I won't dob you in. Somebody probably should, but it won't be me. Dr Crusoe got those *kadaicha* boots because she helped people. But you're so selfish, you think you can just walk in and take them. I think you're pathetic.'

'Me? Selfish? Pathetic? You can talk,' sneered Marie-Claire. 'The only time you help someone is if you can get something out of it. Like with your sister, you only helped her to make yourself feel good, and when she wasn't grateful enough you got all high and mighty. You sit around judging people, waiting for them to do the right thing by you. Me, your sister, even your big brother,

146

you think everyone else should come back to you without you having to do a thing. You just wait for someone else to try, and then you stick it to them when it's not the way you want it. No wonder your family call you Bubs. You're just a big baby. You're boring.'

'If I'm so boring, why are you here? Why don't you go back to your precious Tracy Grogan?'

'At least if I gave Tracy a present, even if it wasn't the right thing, she'd say thanks. She'd understand I'm trying.'

'That present wasn't for me. It was for you. You nicked those boots because you think if you want something, you should have it. As if you're somebody special, some sort of bloody princess.'

'I stole them for you,' said Marie-Claire, her voice suddenly quiet. She looked down at the *kadaicha* boots and gently pulled out a single feather.

'No you didn't,' said PJ, blinking back tears. 'You were only thinking of yourself – Miss Know-it-all Marie-Claire. If you'd thought about me, you never would have stolen them!'

PJ wrenched open the door and jumped out into seawater. The tide had come right in all along the beach and water swirled around the stumps of the bathing box. She ran along the beach, with tears streaming down her face. She didn't look back to see if Marie-Claire was watching. She didn't care anymore.

21

Imagining proof

Mum didn't notice PJ's tear-streaked face. She was lying on the couch with a folded hanky across her eyes. On the little table beside her was a packet of Bex, the white powder spilling across the dark wood veneer of the table.

'Is that you, Pauline?' she asked. 'I'm just having a little lie-down, love. Got one of my migraines again. Could you draw the curtains for me, there's a pet.'

PJ padded across the carpet and slid the heavy dark curtains across. Outside, in the back garden, Dad was watering the hydrangeas, even though it had started to rain. He had a numb, miserable expression on his face that PJ could hardly bear to look at.

There was no one she could talk to. She went to her room and sat on the white chenille coverlet, picking at the threads. It was as if everything was broken in pieces and she didn't know how to glue it all back together again. Just when she thought she was going to start crying again, there was a loud miaow behind her. Friday was sitting on the bedroom windowsill, staring in at her. PJ slid the window open and the big cat leapt onto her bed.

'You shouldn't be in here,' said PJ. 'Mum hates cats.' But she pulled Friday onto her lap anyway. Friday started purring. PJ could feel the rich, warm sound vibrating through both their bodies.

'You and me, we're the only ones around here that haven't changed,' she said miserably, stroking Friday's thick black fur. 'Marie-Claire has gone bananas. She says I sit around waiting for everyone else to do everything for me but it's not fair and it's not true. I can't figure out everything all by myself. I don't know what I'm meant to do!'

Friday turned her face up, and looked at PJ.

'Well, at least I know what I can do to help you,' said PJ, sighing.

She pushed Friday off her lap and went into the kitchen to fetch a bowl of milk.

The letter was lying face down on the kitchen table. As soon as she saw it, PJ knew it was from Brian. She glanced over her shoulder, to be sure no one was near. On either side of the letter was an empty tea-cup. Mum and Dad must have been reading it over morning tea.

PJ picked up the envelope and turned it over in her hands. There it was, Brian's address written in neat handwriting on the back of the letter. It only took her a moment to memorise it. She ran back to her room and scribbled it on a scrap of paper. Friday looked up at her curiously.

'I've got it!' she said to the cat. 'And this time, I know what to do.'

It was a long way from Hampton to St Kilda. PJ followed the beach road, figuring eventually she'd find Luna Park. As she cycled through Elwood, the flares of her jeans caught in the bicycle chain and the bike came down hard against the kerb. A man in a white Valiant leaned on his horn as she dragged the bike up onto the footpath and disentangled the black and greasy denim. Suddenly, she wasn't so sure that she was doing the right thing. What if Brian had changed too? Maybe she should give up now, go home and wait for things to get better. She was turning her bike around when something Dr Crusoe had said came back to her: *Those who restrain desire, do so because theirs is weak enough to be restrained.* It galvanised her into action. She flung one leg over the bike and started pedalling towards St Kilda as fast as she could.

The clouds lifted and the winter sunshine was warm on her back as she passed St Kilda marina and caught sight of the white web of framing that supported the Scenic Railway at Luna Park. Brian's flat was down the street that ran behind it. The high walls of the fun park cast a shadow across the street and into the tiny patch of garden at the front of his building. PJ leaned her bike against the wall inside the entrance and rang the bell.

Julie opened the door.

'Pauline!'

'Hi,' said PJ in a small voice, suddenly shy.

Julie peered over PJ's shoulder, looking to see if anyone was with her.

'Well . . .' said Julie. 'This is a nice surprise.'

'Yeah,' said PJ, her mouth dry. 'I need to talk to Brian.'

'Brian's not here. Is there something you want me to tell him? A message from your parents?'

PJ scrunched up her face and shifted from foot to foot.

'I really need to talk to him,' she said.

Julie looked perplexed. 'He won't be back for a while, and I was about to go out too. But look, why don't you come in and hang around until Brian comes home?'

PJ hesitated, glancing back down the path to where she'd left her bicycle. This wasn't working out quite the way she'd envisioned.

'Does your mum know you're here?' asked Julie, following PJ's anxious gaze.

'Nope. You know, she reckons you're living in sin and we can't visit you.'

Julie reached out and touched PJ lightly on the arm.

'Then I guess it was a big deal for you to come here. Thanks for that. Are you coming into the sin-bin or not?'

Ten minutes later, Julie was gone, and PJ was sitting on a big orange beanbag, waiting for Brian's return. The flat was warm and dark. Against one wall was an old club lounge covered with a crocheted rug, and the windowsill was lined with plants. Every inch of wall space was covered with posters and political flyers, even in the tiny galley kitchen. A wisp of smoke rose up from an incense burner. PJ got up and wandered around the room, picking things up and putting them back in place carefully. It was almost like playing Marie-Claire's visiting game. She felt a stab of grief at the thought of Marie-Claire. She knew she'd never play the visiting game with her again.

In a nook of the old brick verandah, now enclosed with louvred windows, was a double bed covered with a big bright patchwork quilt. PJ lay down on it and traced the patterns on the different squares of the patchwork. If she looked up she could see the Scenic Railway through the windows, high against the pale blue winter sky. Every so often the carriages rattled past. Beyond the whirling noises of the fun park were the sounds of traffic and the sea.

PJ hadn't even realised she'd fallen asleep until she felt a prickle of whiskers against her cheek. She opened her eyes and saw Brian.

'Hey, little sister,' he said.

'Brian, you're so hairy!' exclaimed PJ.

'She doesn't like the beard,' he called out to Julie, who was in the kitchen.

'Tell her a kiss without a beard is like an egg without salt,' called Julie.

'Hear that?' he said.

'I think I like my eggs plain,' said PJ.

Brian had grown a goatee beard and a moustache, and his hair was longer than ever, tied back from his face in a ponytail. He wore bright pink flares and a purple shirt. PJ thought he looked like a rock'n'roll star from the cover of a record album.

Suddenly, PJ noticed that outside the louvred windows the sky was tinged with orange streaks, and the lights were starting to come on in Luna Park.

'Oh no,' she wailed. 'It's so late and I have so much to tell you and now there's no time. I'm going to have to get on my bike and go home or Mum and Dad will go bananas.'

'Whoa! Slow down, Bubs. Don't panic. Why don't we walk down to the phone booth on the corner and call them up?'

'Because they'll flip out if they know I'm here!' said PJ.

'Then I'll talk to them!' said Brian. He grabbed PJ by the hand and dragged her off the bed.

PJ waited outside the red phone box, listening with one ear pushed against the cold glass. She couldn't believe it. Brian explained to Mum that he'd bring PJ home after they'd had tea together, and he didn't even have to shout.

PJ skipped all the way back to the flat. At the front door, Brian turned her around to face him. 'Look, Pauline. I don't know what Mum and Dad told you about me and Julie, but I love her and I don't accept that stuff about living in sin. I'm living in love!'

Julie cooked up some weird vegetarian dish that PJ couldn't really stomach. PJ sat on the club lounge with the plate on her lap – there was no proper table to sit at. She pushed the food around while she told Brian about everything that had been happening at home, about Sue running away and Mum always having a headache and Dad always being so sad, and how she hated being an only child. She didn't tell him anything about Marie-Claire. That was still too raw inside her. Brian listened intently, his dark eyes serious. When she got to the part about using her newspaper earnings to buy bags of food for Sue, Brian reached out and took one of PJ's hands in his.

'You've had a lot on your plate, haven't you, Bubs?' he said softly.

PJ looked guiltily at her food. When it dawned on her what he meant, she said, 'Well, what do you think we should do about Sue?'

'I don't know. If she won't listen to you, she probably won't listen to me either. But I'll see what I can do.'

'I promised her I wouldn't tell anyone where she lived, but I don't think I should have.'

'Don't worry, Bubs. I'll tell her I heard it on the grapevine.'

'By the way, Brian, nobody calls me Bubs anymore. PJ, that's what I want to be called.'

'PJ?'

'You know, Pauline Janet.'

'My baby sister is growing up. Do you reckon you're too grown-up for Luna Park, PJ?' said Brian, trying to look serious.

'I'll never be that grown-up,' said PJ.

'Me neither,' said Julie.

'You're on, both of you. Luna Park it is,' said Brian.

They cleared away the dishes and stepped out into the cool night air. Luna Park was lit up, with the Scenic Railway carriages making a blur of light as they sped down into a dark tunnel. PJ looked up at the laughing-mouth entrance and laughed herself. The fight with Marie-Claire seemed like a bad dream now. Brian bought three cream-filled waffles, one for each of them, and they walked down towards the Giggle Palace, stuffing their faces with the rich, creamy treat. The King of Laughter nodded down at them from his throne and they climbed up into the heart of the Palace. They screamed down the slippery slides until they felt bruised and breathless. Julie didn't want to go on the Big Dipper in case she couldn't keep the waffle down. PJ liked the Scenic Railway better anyway. She could feel the seabreeze turning her cheeks pink as the roller-coaster carriages arced around the edge of the park, high above the crowds. A shimmer of gold stretched across the black waters and far away the pinprick lights of Corio Bay shone like distant fairy castles in the darkness.

In the Penny Arcade, they crammed into a photo booth and PJ sat on Julie and Brian's knees so her face loomed large at the front of the picture, while behind her Julie and Brian leaned their heads together and stuck their tongues out.

'Better not let Mum see that. She might worry that we're leading you astray, giving you wrong ideas. Speaking of the old girl, I told her I'd get you back before ten o'clock. I want to show her even us sinners can be reliable, so we'd better skidaddle.'

'Just one last thing,' said PJ. She ran up to the booth of the gypsy fortune-teller and slipped a 20-cent piece into the slot. The dark red curtain parted and slowly the wax dummy of the gypsy fortune-teller raised her head, her hands hovering over her crystal ball. PJ thought it was the creepiest thing she'd ever seen, but she couldn't resist trying it. She stared into the black glass eyes of the mannequin. A minute later, it spat out a card with her fortune printed on it in tiny lettering: *What is now proved was once, only imagin'd.*

Julie took the tiny card from her and read it. 'What a rip-off. What's that meant to mean? It's the strangest one I've ever read,' she said, frowning. 'I thought they said things like, "Tomorrow you'll be rich and famous".'

'It's by William Blake,' said PJ tucking it into her jeans pocket carefully. 'It means coming down to St Kilda to see you guys was a good idea. It means I imagined us being together and now I've proved it can happen.'

Julie and Brian looked at each other, astonished.

'Since when did you read William Blake?'

'Since you went away. You used to say if you're not part of the solution, you're part of the problem. I figured it was about time I solved something.'

22

Broken doors

PJ heard Mum leave for church. Dad was moving slowly, heavily, around the kitchen, and the kettle whistled a long, loud blast. PJ went out and stood at the kitchen table as he sat with a cup of tea and yesterday's papers.

'Were you mad at me, for going to see Brian and Julie?' asked PJ.

Dad just shook the newspaper and cleared his throat. PJ gently took a corner of the paper and pulled it back so she could see his face.

'Dad?'

'No, love. I'm not cross with you. He's your brother, even if he's not much of a man. I s'pose you've got a right to see him, if you want.'

'Mum was pretty angry, though, wasn't she?'

'Well, you know, love, she's worried you'll get the wrong ideas.'

'I don't understand a lot of Brian's ideas but I don't reckon they're all wrong – they're just different. But I had to see Brian for a special reason. It wasn't about me. It's Sue.'

Dad put the newspaper down and looked at PJ hard. 'What about Sue?'

'I've been visiting her too.'

'You know where she's living?' he asked.

PJ nodded. 'She's in trouble. She's got really skinny and she looks sick all the time. I talked to Brian about it, but then I thought you ought to know too 'cause Brian said you should, but I said I couldn't tell you because I'd promised Sue. Then I lay awake for ages last night. I couldn't figure out what was more important – the truth or the promise. Brian said that even though he didn't agree with everything you and Mum thought about politics and all, he knew you loved all your kids and wanted good things for them. So if you love Sue and want things to be good for her, I think you'd better do something.'

Dad looked pale as he and PJ stepped up onto the battered front verandah of Sue's house. A cat leapt down from a tree that overhung the path and PJ nearly jumped out of her skin.

Fuzz opened the door and groaned at the sight of them.

'What is this? More of the bloody McArdle mafia?' he

said and turned away, disappearing into one of the bedrooms.

'C'mon,' said PJ and led the way into the gloomy hallway. A big sheet of wallpaper had been half peeled off the wall and lay dangling across the floor. Dad shook his head.

A man was kneeling in the doorway of Sue's room.

'You!' said Dad. He stepped in front of PJ and glared at the man.

'Doug,' said Brian, standing up and dusting sawdust from the front of his pink overalls.

'What are you doing here?'

'Some animal kicked Sue's door in. I was fixing it for her. She's nipped out to get some milk.'

'You? Fixing something? Here, let me take a look,' said Dad, touching the splintered wood and twisted hinges of Sue's bedroom door.

'I know what I'm doing,' said Brian, folding his arms across his chest

'You won't fix it with that old brace and bit,' said Dad, nudging the tool with his foot.

'Look, I know it's a lousy tool. I'd use a power drill if I had one.'

'You wouldn't know how to use one anyway,' said Dad. 'Leave it to me. I can sort this.'

'Actually,' said Brian between gritted teeth, 'I do know how to use one, no thanks to you. You only ever let me use your crappiest hand tools. It's amazing I learnt anything, but I do know how to do this and I don't need you to show me.'

Dad picked up the tool from the floor. 'I gave you this, didn't I?' he said, turning the hand drill over in his hand. 'You don't understand, boy. You've got to start with the old tools. If you can't use the old tools, you're not any sort of tradesman.'

Brian rolled his eyes. 'Don't call me boy, Doug.'

'Dad, Brian,' said PJ pleadingly. 'Don't fight. That's not what we're here for!'

'Yeah,' said Brian. 'I'm here for Sue. Someone's got to help her and you haven't been interested in doing it.'

'We did our best,' said Dad, defensively. 'First, we hoped she'd come home when she was good and ready but then, after your mum saw her like a wild thing in the street, I started searching for her high and low. Just couldn't run her to ground. She's as proud and stubborn as her mother.'

There was a crash of glass. Sue stood at the back door, glass and milk splattering across the wooden floor. 'PJ!' she shouted. 'You promised! You promised!'

Tears and streaks of black mascara ran down her face as she knelt to pick up the fragments of the broken milk bottle.

Dad stepped forward and put his hand up like a policeman signalling stop.

'Suzy, I just wanted to see you. To see that you're alright. See your new home, love.'

'About time,' muttered Brian, under his breath.

'Go away,' sobbed Sue. 'All of you. I don't want any of you here. Get out!'

Dad followed Sue into the kitchen and tried to put his arms around her, but she pushed him away.

'Get out!' she shrieked.

Five minutes later, Brian, PJ and Dad were standing outside in the street, staring at the closed front door.

'Now, look what you've done, the pair of you!' said PJ. She stormed across the street and climbed back into the car, slumping down in the front seat. She could hear Dad and Brian arguing, shouting at each other as they stood outside Sue's front gate. She turned the radio on and slumped even lower so she couldn't see them. What was *wrong* with her family?

After ten minutes she realised the voices had stopped. She looked up and down the street. Dad and Brian were standing in front of the open boot of Brian's Volkswagen. Dad had one hand on Brian's shoulder – and they were both smiling.

'What's going to happen?' PJ asked Dad, as he eased himself back into the front seat.

'Brian's got a bit of a plan. He's going to get his lass, Julie, to come and have a word with Sue. If Julie can talk her round, they'll all come down to our place for tea. May not be much of a handyman, that boy, but he thinks about things.'

PJ smiled, but then a worrying thought came to her. 'What about Mum?'

'I'll sort it, love. I know she comes across a bit hard sometimes, but underneath it she's a softy, your mum.'

PJ was standing in the hallway when Mum opened the front door that evening. The moths flitted around the outside lamp and into the house. Standing in the glowing circle of light was Sue.

'Suzy,' said Mum. Her body was so stiff, so rigid, that for a minute PJ was afraid she was going to say something angry or shut the door again, but all of a sudden she stepped forward and put her arms around Sue. 'My little girl,' she said.

Julie followed them into the house and PJ saw Mum reach out and touch her on the arm.

'Thank you,' she said.

'It was nothing,' said Julie.

They sat around the kitchen table and PJ helped Mum make cups of tea for everyone. It was as if they were all raw and tender, like a family of snails without shells, and they had to be careful not to wound each other. The conversation was subdued, punctuated with silences and short bursts of laughter, as the light outside the window faded and night crept over.

'I'd like you all to stay for dinner, but I haven't fixed anything,' said Mum.

'Don't worry about that, we don't need a roast dinner,' said Dad. 'How about Brian and me nip down to the Chinese – takeaway for everyone, eh?'

Mum didn't really approve of takeaway food, but she nodded and looked around the table at all the faces, at last, a table full of faces after all these quiet months.

'We'll set the table in the dining room, won't we, girls?' she said, looking from Julie to Sue and PJ. 'We'll use the good crockery and Granny's Irish linen.'

PJ ran her hand across the smooth white tablecloth and watched as Dad piled her plate high with fried rice and lemon chicken. Sue was already eating, not just picking at the food, but laughing at some joke Julie had made and loading her fork up with sweet and sour pork. Brian caught PJ's eye and winked. 'Feels like the tide is turning, hey, PJ?'

'And the surf's definitely up,' said PJ as she lifted her glass of lemonade in a toast.

23

The whole truth

PJ stood on Dr Crusoe's back doorstep and banged the side of Friday's bowl. A light rain pattered on the tangled undergrowth but no cat emerged. PJ banged louder and felt a mixture of guilt and crankiness. Things had been so upside-down since the fight with Marie-Claire and the excitement of getting Sue and Brian back home, that she hadn't been over to feed Friday for two days. After waiting for twenty minutes, PJ emptied the food into Friday's bowl and set it down by the back step.

On Tuesday afternoon, the paper round seemed to take forever. PJ kept shooting past some of the houses on her list, she was so caught up with other thoughts.

PJ remembered waking that morning to the sound of Dad whistling in the kitchen. It made her realise how long it was since she'd heard him sounding happy. Mum had a brightness about her that made PJ want to hug her.

She couldn't believe how quickly things had turned around. When she dropped by Sue's house, she found Julie and Brian helping Sue clear her room out. Sue was moving back home.

But underneath her happiness, PJ felt a swelling sense of unease. Marie-Claire hadn't been at school the last couple of days and PJ swung wildly from never wanting to see her again to wanting to have it out with her as soon as possible. In her imagination, she played out a dozen different scenes where she would confront Marie-Claire in the schoolyard and announce her success in bringing her family together. Last night she'd dreamt they were both in the bathing box, surrounded by wild seas, shouting at each other over the roar of the ocean.

PJ was still running through a variation of her stick-it-to-Marie-Claire scenarios when she turned into Kenneth Street and braked hard. Dr Crusoe was getting out of a taxi with her bags. She waved at PJ, but PJ pretended not to notice and fiddled with the front tyre of her bike, as if it was giving her problems. When Dr Crusoe pushed open her garden gate and disappeared up the path, PJ breathed a sigh of relief.

PJ dropped her bike by the back door and hurried inside.

'Mum,' she called. 'Mum, have you seen Dr Crusoe's cat around, you know, the big black one that looks like a stray?'

Mum was in the laundry, loading a pile of Sue's clothes into the machine. 'No, dear, I haven't noticed it about.'

PJ grimaced. 'I'm in big trouble,' she muttered to herself and ran outside again. She climbed the back fence and walked along the top rail like a tightrope walker, scanning the adjoining back yards for a glimpse of Friday. When that failed, she got back on her bike and cycled around the block, looking in every garden, calling down the bumpy back lanes.

That evening, PJ couldn't eat her tea. Every noise made her jump, she was so anxious that Dr Crusoe would come to the door and ask about Friday – or worse, ask if the McArdles knew anything about who had burgled her house. PJ went straight to her room after tea and lay on her bed, staring at the ceiling.

There was a knock at the bedroom door. 'Is everything alright, Pauline?' asked Mum, coming into the room and sitting down on the bed beside PJ.

'Fine,' said PJ.

'I've just had a very worrying phone call from the mother of a friend of yours, Margaret. The girl's been missing since Saturday.'

PJ frowned. 'Margaret? I don't know any Margaret.'

'Of course you do. Margaret – that tall lass with the dark curly hair. She was in and out of our house all last summer. She called herself that odd name – what was it?'

'Marie-Claire!' gasped PJ, sitting up.

Mum started to untie her apron.

'That's right – Marie-Claire. The school gave out a list of people who were her friends and you were on it. The police have been notified and they're going to be at the Tierneys this evening to make out a report. I told Mrs Tierney I'd bring you over to talk to them.'

'Why me? Why don't they talk with Tracy Grogan instead? She's been hanging out with Marie . . . Margaret, more than me.'

'Tracy Grogan? Alan and Marjorie's girl? We were playing bowls with them last Saturday. I heard they packed Tracy off to boarding school a week ago, so she's not going to be able to help the Tierneys. Poor things, they're out of their minds with worry. Margaret's only thirteen. I don't know what I would have done if we'd had that sort of trouble with Sue when she was that young. Bad enough when she was seventeen.'

PJ slumped in the front seat of the car as they drove over to the Tierneys'. All those months they'd walked home together and Marie-Claire had never let PJ come near her house. And now she'd be seeing it without Marie-Claire being there, without even knowing where Marie-Claire was. It felt all wrong.

The house was in a small side street that ran along the railway line. It wasn't like any of the versions that Marie-Claire had described. It was a drab brick veneer with no garden – a flat, bleak lawn, no trees and a few hydrangeas and azaleas clumped around the fences.

'This can't be Marie-Claire's house,' said PJ.

Mum checked the note she'd written the address on. 'Well, it is.'

Mr Tierney answered the door. He was a big, powerful man, and his body almost filled the door frame. He was much older than PJ had imagined him to be, and his face was lined and weathered. He looked as if he could have been Marie-Claire's grandfather, rather than her dad. Mrs Tierney was sitting in the tiny back kitchen, nursing a cup of tea. She had long grey hair tied back in a bun, and more wrinkles than PJ thought anyone's mother should have. A young police officer was filling in the details of a long form.

Mr Tierney ushered PJ and her mum into the kitchen and offered them each a chair.

'Thanks for coming by,' said Mr Tierney. His accent didn't sound Russian. It was more like an Aussie shearer's than a White Russian prince-cum-brain surgeon's.

'We know it's been hard for Margie, coming down here from the country,' said Mrs Tierney. 'She was always out riding her pony through the bush or off on some adventure on our property. It's been hard for all of us but hardest for Margie.'

'So she *has* got a pony,' said PJ, relieved that at least that detail of Marie-Claire's stories was true.

Mrs Tierney put one hand to her chest, as if she was in pain. 'We should have worked out a way for her to keep Silver. But we had to sell all the livestock along with the farm. We'd been running at a loss for too long. We'd always hoped to keep the place together for our boy Kev to take on, but when he came back from Vietnam, well, there wasn't much hope of that.'

Mrs Tierney lowered her voice and her face looked even more careworn.

'Margie took it all so hard. You see, our boy, the Kevin we waved off on the troopship, he wasn't the boy who came home to us. Kev got wounded by a landmine – his best mate was killed and Kev lost his right arm and was blinded in one eye. You can't expect a lad to be the same after that and little Margie, she just found it too much. I know that's been the hardest thing of all for her. When she was a tiny tot she worshipped Kev, and to find him like he is now . . .' She folded her hands around her cup of tea.

Mr Tierney reached across and touched his wife gently on the arm.

'You see, we had to bring Kev to the city so he could get the right treatment,' said Mr Tierney, 'And we thought it would be good for Margaret too. But we haven't been able to keep enough of an eye on her. I work nights as a watchman so I'm asleep during the day, and Alice, she's been working two jobs, trying to make ends meet, help pay off our debts.'

'Oh Bill,' said Mrs Tierney. 'It's not only that. She's had such trouble making friends except for your Pauline. When she didn't come home on Saturday night, we thought she'd got herself on a train back to the bush.

She's done that before. So we went after her – drove all the way up there. But no one had seen hide nor hair of the lass.'

'I haven't seen much of Marie – Margaret – lately either,' said PJ. She picked at a loose thread at the hem of her uniform and tried not to meet anyone's gaze.

The young policeman turned his attention to PJ.

'When was the last time you saw Margaret?' he asked, his pen poised above the paper.

'Saturday morning,' said PJ, without looking up. 'Around eleven, I think.'

Mrs Tierney drew a sharp breath. 'We haven't seen her since Saturday breakfast. Where was she, Pauline?'

PJ squirmed uncomfortably in her seat. 'On the beach, just down from the Burnham Street entrance.' She could feel her heart beating faster.

'Was there anyone else with you, and did Margaret give any indication of what her plans were?' asked the police officer.

'Umm, no just us two. And she didn't say much. But there was a man and a dog further along the beach.' Out of the corner of her eye, PJ saw the officer note down this detail, and she blushed. She knew it was a red herring.

'And how do you think Margaret was feeling? Was she upset about anything?'

'She seemed okay to me,' said PJ slowly. 'I only stayed a little while and then I came home. I think she planned to stay on the beach on her own a bit longer. I don't know anything else. Can I go and wait outside now? I'd kind of like some fresh air.'

Mum glanced across at the police officer and the Tierneys, questioningly.

'Can you think of anything you can add that might help us to locate Margaret?' asked the policeman.

PJ shook her head and slipped out of her chair. 'Can I go now?' she pleaded.

The policeman nodded and PJ looked at her mother. 'I won't be a minute, Pauline,' said Mum. 'Wait on the front verandah.'

The dark winter night had come down. PJ pushed open the front door and stepped outside. A man was leaning against the black wrought-iron verandah post. He had long dark hair tied back in a ponytail and he was smoking a cigarette. The smouldering orange tip dimly illuminated his scarred face.

'Hey, kid,' he said, without glancing at PJ.

'Are you Kevin?' asked PJ.

'Yeah,' he said. He dropped his cigarette butt onto the concrete verandah and ground it out with the heel of his boot. PJ stared at him, feeling all her anger towards Marie-Claire well up inside her again. How could she have told PJ so many lies?

'Your sister told me you were killed in Vietnam,' she blurted out.

Kevin didn't say anything. He took a packet of tobacco out of his coat pocket and deftly rolled another cigarette using his left hand. The right sleeve of his coat hung limp and empty beside him, a black shadow where his hand should have been.

'She said you died saving your mate and a bunch of kids and that the government had given her all your medals. Why do you reckon she lied like that?'

'I reckon you weren't much of a friend to her if she couldn't tell you the truth,' he replied, his voice thick with anger.

PJ took a step back. For a moment, she thought Kevin was about to turn on her and shout. She fumbled for the front door knob. Suddenly, the door swung open and her mother was standing on the threshold with Mr and Mrs Tierney behind her, thanking her and PJ for coming over.

PJ couldn't get in the car fast enough. All the way home Mum talked about how nice the Tierneys were, until PJ wanted to cover her ears and scream, *They're not nice. They're horrible and Marie-Claire's the worst of them because she's such a liar! I hate them all.* Instead, she folded her arms across her chest and looked out the window at the ring of distant lights that embraced the black waters of the bay.

24

All the lies

When the car pulled into the drive, the headlights showed Dr Crusoe walking out the McArdles' front gate, as if she'd just been visiting. PJ crouched down in the seat and hid. The last person she felt like facing at that moment was Dr Crusoe.

'Pauline, the old biddy from next door came by. Says she wants a word with you,' said Dad, opening the door to them. 'You'd better nip round there quick smart and then straight back home and into bed.'

PJ felt a rush of panic. How could she look Dr Crusoe in the eye with Friday and the *kadaicha* boots missing?

'Go on,' said Mum. 'She probably just wants to thank you for looking after that cat of hers or ask where you've put the tin-opener.'

PJ trudged up the path to Dr Crusoe's and rang the doorbell.

'Miss McArdle. Thank you for coming. I got back this afternoon and there's something I'm rather worried about. Come inside from the cold.'

She followed Dr Crusoe into the living room. The first thing she saw was the *kadaicha* boots, sitting on the mantel on either side of the old French clock.

'The *kadaicha* boots!' she exclaimed. 'What are they doing there?'

'I haven't had a chance to rehang them properly,' said Dr Crusoe. 'Perhaps you know that while I was away, someone broke into my house and took a number of things. I was very perplexed, obviously, and searched the house trying to ascertain what exactly was missing before I reported it to the police. Then, you wouldn't believe it, I was upstairs checking the bedroom when I heard someone rattling the back door. I thought it might have been you, but when I went to the window and called out, whoever it was hurried away – simply disappeared into the under-growth of the garden – and by the time I got downstairs they were gone. And on the back doorstep was a cardboard box. Inside were all the things that had been stolen, with this note on top of them.' She handed PJ a piece of paper.

In bright red ink was a single word. 'Sorry.' It was written in Marie-Claire's fancy curling handwriting.

'I don't think they realised I was home. I thought perhaps they'd been watching the house and seen you come in to feed Friday and hoped to find the key, but it wasn't under the brick where we usually hide it.'

175

PJ handed back the note.

'Gee,' she said. Her hands were trembling and she tucked them under her armpits to make them be still.

'The key, Miss McArdle?'

'Oh, right. I took it home with me. It's safe. I didn't want to leave it in the old place after . . .'

All of a sudden, PJ couldn't keep it in any longer. Out it all came, about Marie-Claire and the visiting game and the whole history of her friendship with Margaret 'Marie-Claire' Tierney. When she got to the end, of visiting the Tierneys' house that evening and finally hearing the truth, she could barely contain her rage.

'And so I told her brother, told him how she had lied about him being dead, and you know what? He was really rude to me. But it wasn't me who started all the troubles. She was the liar, not me! She lied about everything!'

Dr Crusoe's expression clouded and she measured her words carefully as she spoke. 'Do you mean to tell me, that you told your friend's brother that she had denied him? The poor man. You must have realised he'd be hurt by knowing that his sister had felt the need to make up a story about him. What were you thinking?'

'I was thinking that someone had to tell the truth!' said PJ, almost shouting. 'I was thinking he should know what a creep his sister is.'

'My dear girl,' said Dr Crusoe, 'our friend Mr Blake said *A truth that's told with bad intent, beats all the lies one can invent.* It was not a kindness to tell this young man about his sister's invention.'

'Well, aren't you going to call the police and tell them what she did? How she stole your things?'

'But she brought them back. She obviously has a conscience and, I suspect, a good heart, even if her imagination is a little over-active. I feel concerned for her. I don't wish to add to her burdens and neither should you. I should like to reassure her that I bear her no ill will. I would appreciate it if you could tell her that, from me.'

'But I can't tell her!' shouted PJ, bursting into tears. 'I don't know where she is!' Hot angry tears of frustration and grief poured down her cheeks. Suddenly Dr Crusoe's arms were around her, guiding her to the couch, where she sat down heavily among the cushions.

'I've lost Friday too,' sobbed PJ, great hiccuping breaths choking her.

Dr Crusoe sighed. 'You mustn't mind about Friday. She's a tough old creature. She'll come home when she's ready. It's your little friend that we must pray for, not my wicked old alley cat.'

PJ lay in bed staring at the dark ceiling. Why hadn't Marie-Claire told her? Why hadn't she told her the truth? PJ felt she had to scrub out all the pictures she had in her head of the old Marie-Claire and replace them with a stranger, and each time she had to change something about the Marie-Claire she thought she knew, she grew more confused. Maybe it was her fault. Maybe everyone was right to be angry with her. Maybe she hadn't been a good enough friend. It took ages to fall asleep, and when she did, her dreams were full of strange and horrible images.

She was on the beach but it wasn't the beach she knew. It seemed to stretch forever, but far away, shimmering in the distance, she could just make out a small building – the bathing box. The sand was black and sticky, and a strange smoke was rising up from it. It stuck to her feet as she ran, trying to reach the bathing box. But the faster she ran, the further away the bathing box became. Suddenly, a wall of fire rose up in front of her. She could hear screaming from the other side of the flames, and just as she was about to turn away from the blaze, a big black panther leapt through the fire, knocking her down into the wet sand. She woke bathed in sweat, to the sound of an unearthly scream shuddering up through her body. But it wasn't her own voice that she heard. She sat up in the dark and fumbled for the bedside lamp, but even with the light switched on, the screaming didn't stop.

She ran down the hall to her parents' bedroom in her bare feet and pushed open the door. Mum sat up in bed and stared at her.

'There's something spooky in my room,' said PJ in a small voice, feeling like a baby.

Somehow, PJ had imagined the screaming would stop when Mum came into the room, but it went on and on, more like a weird animal wail than a human scream. Together they lifted the bedspread and looked under the bed. Then Mum smiled.

'I think I know where that missing cat of yours has got to,' she said. She led PJ into the kitchen and took a flash-light from the cupboard. Then together they stepped out into the night. PJ couldn't believe how brave her mum was being. She knelt on the concrete path that ran under the bedroom window and gestured for PJ to do the same. It was cold, and their breath made clouds of mist as they knelt side by side.

'Here, look,' she said, shining the torch at the house. PJ knelt down beside her, peering through the cracks in the base boards. A pair of glowing green eyes shone in the flashlight beam. Directly underneath PJ's bedroom floor, Friday lay curled around a pair of small, damp, wriggling creatures.

'She's had *kittens*,' said PJ, astonished.

'Yes, the poor old thing,' said Mum, dusting the dirt from her knees. 'Cats do like a nice warm dry place to have their babies. And she looks done in from the effort. Let's slip a saucer of milk in there for her, help her get her strength back.'

'Shouldn't we take her out from under the house and bring the kittens inside?' asked PJ hopefully.

'No, I think she'll be very protective of them just now. Let's leave her to get to know her babies in peace.'

In the kitchen, Mum warmed up some milk in a pot

and poured some into a dish for Friday. She used the rest to make hot chocolate for herself and PJ.

'I wonder what Dr Crusoe will say – three cats instead of one!' said PJ. 'I'm so glad we found her. I was dreaming about her when all the noise woke me. I was dreaming . . .'

Suddenly, PJ's dream came back to her, and she saw a face on the other side of the flames, the face that was revealed when the black panther had leapt towards her.

'Mum, I know where Marie-Claire is. I'm so stupid, I should have realised straight away. Oh Mum, please, can we go and find her? I have to find her. I have to find her right now.'

25

On the beach

They drove down along the beach road. The ti-tree scrub clumped thick and dark along the roadside, with small black openings where paths led down to the beach.

'Stop the car, Mum.'

'What?'

'Stop the car here.'

Mum pulled over and PJ leapt out. 'I'll be back in a few minutes. I promise. Just wait here, please, Mum.'

'Oh no you don't. I'm coming with you,' said Mum. But PJ was too fast for her. She ran down the twisting sandy path, scratching her face on the ti-trees as she took a shortcut through the scrub that led straight to the beach. A flicker of light was showing through the cracks in the old bathing-box wall. It was high tide and the beach was under water, small waves lapping at the stumps of the bathing box. PJ had pulled her jeans on over her pyjamas and the double layer of fabric grew heavy with sea water as she ran through the knee-deep tide.

Something was wrong. The light from inside the bathing box was too bright, too strong. PJ smelt the smoke from halfway along the beach. When she reached the bathing box and pushed the door open, Marie-Claire was standing in a ring of fire, beating at the flames with a towel, coughing and gasping.

'Marie-Claire,' PJ called.

Marie-Claire didn't hear her over the crackling of the burning timbers. PJ leapt inside and grabbed the back of Marie-Claire's jumper. She had to shield her face with one hand, the heat was so intense. Little flecks of ash and cinder settled on her clothes.

'You can't save it. It doesn't matter. Get out!'

Marie-Claire looked around, bewildered, numb. PJ dragged her to the door and pushed her out, into the swirling water.

The flames rose up bright against the sky as PJ and Marie-Claire stood watching the bathing box being destroyed by fire. Soon there'd be nothing left to burn. Icy seawater lapped at their feet, and the tide swirled in around the stumps of the bathing box. There was a hissing noise as burning floorboards fell into the sea. The fire lit up the whole beach, sending long orange streaks of light rippling across the surface of the water.

Marie-Claire was wet and shivering.

'I tried to save it,' she said miserably. 'But it was my

own stupid fault. I stubbed out this dumb cigarette butt in a crack in the floor. I thought it was out and all, and then I fell asleep and woke up and the floor was on fire.'

'But what were you doing here? Why'd you run away?'

Marie-Claire shrugged. 'I don't know. I guess I was hoping you'd come back,' she said.

'Me?'

'Yeah, you. I was waiting for you to come back. I knew you would.'

PJ looked away. She didn't know what to say. So many different emotions were churning around inside her. They both stood staring at the burning frame of the bathing box as it shuddered and lurched before tipping over on its side. The flames flared one last time and then died as the water extinguished them.

PJ heard someone calling and turned to see Mum running across the beach towards them.

'Pauline, Margaret!' she cried. 'Oh my goodness, look at you, Margaret. You're shaking like a leaf. You must be freezing.' She took off her cardigan and wrapped it around Marie-Claire. 'We have to get you up to the car right away and take you straight home. Your parents have been worried sick.'

Suddenly, Marie-Claire's knees buckled and she leaned against Mum. 'Sorry, Mrs McArdle,' she said. 'My legs feel all wonky. I think I need to have a little sit-down before I go anywhere.'

PJ couldn't help wondering if this was just another lie.

She helped Mum lead Marie-Claire up onto a stretch of dry sand above the high tide mark, and sat with her while Mum dashed back up the path to fetch a blanket from the car.

'Do you really feel funny or is that another lie?' asked PJ.

'What do you mean?' said Marie-Claire, wrapping her long arms around her knees. She looked more bedraggled than ever.

'I know you're really *Margaret* Tierney, so it's kind of hard to believe anything you say anymore.'

'Huh?'

'You know what I mean. Why did you make up all that stuff – about your mum and dad and your brother?'

'You've met them, haven't you?' said Marie-Claire flatly, pushing a handful of damp hair away from her face.

'Yes.'

Marie-Claire slumped even lower, resting her head on her knees. PJ had to listen hard to hear what she was saying.

'I wanted to make us sound exciting. At first, it was that I wanted you to like me. And then when I found out about your brother, how could I tell you about my brother?'

'Your brother's okay,' said PJ, ashamed that she couldn't sound more convincing.

Marie-Claire turned her face towards PJ. 'My brother is all broken. He went off to Vietnam and he came back all broken. I wish he'd never gone. You said how it was a stupid war and your brother was a sort of hero for not going, so how could I tell you the truth about my brother? When we went to meet him at the airport, there were people waving placards and holding up a page out of a newspaper about women and children being killed. And he was in hospital for ages and when he came out, he took all his medals that they'd given him and threw them in the bin.'

PJ stared at Marie-Claire. Her chest ached. She wanted to stop but there was so much more she didn't understand. 'There were heaps of other things you fibbed about even before I told you about Brian! Like how your mum was an actress and how you had this amazing house.'

'It's alright for you. Your house and your mum are so nice and there's always good things to eat at your place and your dad has a regular job. At my house, I have to tip-toe around all day while Dad sleeps and Mum doesn't have time to make nice things and Kev is always hanging around smoking cigarettes and watching TV. You know, your mum's just like the mum in the Aktavite ads on TV. When I see that ad, I feel so bad for my mum I want to run up and stand between her and the screen. And Dad, he's like a grandpa, not a regular dad, and Kevin – everyone thinks he's cracked. They call him Kooky Kev. It's not just him missing the arm and all – he's angry all the time and he shouts and . . .'

Marie-Claire's teeth were chattering and she was shivering even more, but she went on fiercely.

'You talked about how you went on those marches with your brother and how great it was. Well, I went on one of them too, with Kev. We had to hold up these signs about supporting the soldiers in Vietnam, and people jeered at us. It was horrible. I hate it when people make fun of Kev. It's not his fault, what happened. I want people to like him, to see that he really is a hero, but they don't. I want people to like me too. I only lied to you so you'd be my friend.'

'I would have liked you anyway.'

'You might not have. You didn't need me. You had Jenny and Melinda, and then, in the end, you went back to them.'

'You had Tracy. You didn't need me anymore.'

Marie-Claire groaned. 'I didn't want Tracy instead of you. I wanted us to be like you were with Jenny and Melinda. I thought Tracy was like us – sort of brave and wanting adventures – but it turned out she was really screwed-up. That day at St Moritz was the worst day ever. I saw you there with Jenny and Melinda and I knew you wouldn't want to talk to me. Tracy was a mess. She'd been mucking around with Tony Taylor in the boys' toilets at the rink. It was horrible, and it wasn't romantic or anything. It was yuk. And then there was the fight, and I took her home to her place, and her mum and dad wouldn't let me in, like it was my fault or something. So when she got sent away and you said you'd meet me down here, I was so stoked. I thought I'd got you back. I wanted it to be special but it all turned upside-down. All I wanted was for you to like me.'

'I always liked you,' said PJ, her voice cracking a little as she spoke. 'You're clever and brave and funny and you're better-looking than me and . . .'

'But I'm not your best friend anymore, am I?' asked Marie-Claire.

PJ frowned, staring out over the black water. 'I don't deserve to be your best friend,' she said. 'We had a deal. We'd signed our names in blood that we'd be loyal forever. I wasn't loyal to you, like I promised, and I told your brother that you lied about him.'

Marie-Claire put her arm around PJ and they sat close together, listening to the waves and watching the incoming tide flow towards them.

Mum flung a blanket around both of them and they drew the folds of it over their heads and wrapped themselves up tightly. 'You look like twins in there,' said Mum. They looked at each other and laughed.

'Now, Margaret,' said Mum, as they followed her up the sandy path through the ti-trees. 'I telephoned your mother from the phone box on Beach Road, and we're taking you straight home. I think you'll have quite a lot of explaining to do, young lady.'

'You're not going to start calling me Margaret from now on, are you?' whispered Marie-Claire to PJ.

'Not unless you start calling me Pauline,' said PJ.

Marie-Claire smiled, and they linked arms under the blanket.

'Remember how last summer I never let you walk back to my place?'

PJ nodded.

'Well, it will be different now,' said Marie-Claire. 'We can walk all the way home together any time you like.'

'Just like best friends,' said PJ.

'What are you two whispering about?' asked Mum as she unlocked the car.

'Nothing much,' said PJ. 'Just how every day from now on, I'll be walking home with Marie-Claire.'

Forever after

'I like this bit here,' said PJ. *I was angry with my friend, I told my wrath, my wrath did end.*'

Marie-Claire snorted. 'Typical, *Pauline*, you always have to be cranky about something, don't you?'

PJ laughed. 'It's poetry, *Margaret!*'

PJ and Marie-Claire were sitting on the floor in PJ's bedroom, with two kittens and a book of William Blake's poetry between them. Dr Crusoe had given it to PJ. It was called *Songs of Innocence and of Experience*. The black-and-white kitten jumped onto the book and batted the pages with its paw. PJ stroked the ginger-and-white fur of the other kitten, nestling in her lap.

Marie-Claire lifted the black-and-white kitten off the pages of the book and held it up admiringly. 'I'm gonna call mine Wednesday, 'cause she's just like Wednesday out of the Addams family with her little white collar and face and all the rest black. Are you still going to call yours Monday?'

'Nah,' said PJ, smiling down at her new pet. 'She's called "Ruby Tuesday" 'cause she changes every day.'

'Not like you?'

PJ smiled knowingly.

'Hey, you two cat-women,' said Sue, sticking her head in around the door. 'Have you got any stickytape in here? I want to put up some more posters.'

'You're not taking down that big one of Che Guevara, are you? Brian really liked that one.'

'Well, it's not Brian's room anymore, is it? It's mine. But don't panic. Che's too sexy to get rid of,' she said. 'Not that I want to get too settled, mind. It's not as if I'm going to be here all that long. I'll hang in until after the wedding, but then I'm out of here.'

'What wedding?' asked Marie-Claire.

'Didn't I tell you? Julie and Brian are getting married. Brian's had a whole suit made out of denim and Julie's got this floaty white cheesecloth sort of caftan. She looks like an angel in it.'

'Hang on, I thought you said Brian and Julie didn't believe in marriage.'

'I don't think they do, but Mum and Dad and Julie's parents had a big go at them. And besides, they're having a baby.'

'Wow! You're going to be an auntie! Auntie Bubs! I wish Kevin would get married some day. I'd like to be an auntie.'

They both went quiet, thinking about Kevin. He hadn't quite forgiven either of them for the trouble they'd caused, but PJ was trying to make it up to him every time she visited Marie-Claire's house.

'Hey, we should get something for Julie and Brian's baby,' said Marie-Claire. 'I saw some really cute things in Myer's. We could go and pick out some special booties, from both of us.'

PJ narrowed her eyes. She wasn't planning on going back to Myer's with Marie-Claire for a while. 'Maybe we could learn to knit. We've got plenty of time.'

Marie-Claire laughed. 'Yup, we've got forever.'

OTHER BOOKS YOU MIGHT LIKE BY KIRSTY MURRAY

Zarconi's Magic Flying Fish

Before he came to Zarconi's, Gus didn't even know he *had* grandparents, let alone ones who juggled knives and ate fire. Now he's caught up in their world of magicians, stilt-walkers, tattooed tenthands, elephant turds – and there's a snake-girl who might become his best friend or his worst enemy. This is Zarconi's Incredible Travelling Circus, and it's full of mysteries. Why is everyone so secretive about Gus's family? Why won't they let him on the trapeze? Is it true that Zarconi's is cursed?

Here's a story of discovery, change and identity, with all the drama of life under the Big Top.

Market Blues

Things unravel so fast. One day Sam is a kid with a straightforward life, next moment he's sucked into a time warp and flung back a hundred years. Meeting Flea, Gertie and the gang in 1901 is just the start of a crazy adventure with Sam on the run from police, sleeping outside the morgue, laying bets on horse races, fighting thieves and larrikins. An accident in a shooting gallery confronts Sam with the hardest decision he's ever had to make. Can he change the past – and his own future?

Market Blues is a fast-moving drama about city kids then and now, about change, choice and history.

Tough Stuff
True stories about kids and courage

From a teenage Olympic champion to the wolf girls of
India; from Iqbal Masih, the inspirational 12-year-old
crusader for human rights to the Dalai Lama; from
outback Australia to Auschwitz, *Tough Stuff* is packed
with true stories that show what kids are really made of.

It's about kids who have protested, prayed, saved lives,
earned a fortune, lost everything, become world-famous,
or survived war and oppression. It's about ordinary kids
doing unbelievable things, and extraordinary kids trying
to live ordinary lives.

Tough Stuff is pacy, poignant, confronting. It speaks
directly to us about things that matter.